Praise for Anna Durand's Books

"[In *One Hot Roomie*] Anna Durand adroitly sets the stage for a fun romantic comedy. [...] Durand's two main characters are perfect foils for each other; both are conflicted and for good reason. Seeing as they try to make being roomies for two weeks work is priceless entertainment."
Jack Magnus, Readers' Favorite

" I loved the slow-burn, should we-shouldn't we, what's right, dilemma and desire that built and built until the steam had to escape. [*One Hot Chance*] is equal parts fun, steam, and moral quandary. [...] I am in love with Chance and his brothers already."
MaryLou Hoffman, Page Princess blog

"[*Lethal in a Kilt* is] full of hot sex, adventure, and so much laughter. I found myself laughing-out-loud at the antics of the Witches of Ballachulish (Logan's sisters) and the hilarious flirting and sexy banter between Serena and Logan. [...] Recommend highly! "
Sharon Clayton, The Eclectic Review

"[*Insatiable in a Kilt*] smokes from the very first pages... Durand's characters are a delight and seeing how they mix business with their increasing attraction for each other is entertaining indeed. [...] Durand's Hot Scots family saga just keeps on getting better."
Readers' Favorite

"I loved the Scottish in Ian and the strength of Rae, but the love of one little girl makes [*Notorious in a Kilt*] something to behold."
Coffee Time Romance

"*Gift-Wrapped in a Kilt* is a marvelous continuation of the author's MacTaggart family saga. Durand's story has an entertaining plot, and her steamy interludes are well-written...a celebration of healthy relationships between loving adults written in a tasteful and compelling manner."
Readers' Favorite

"I have enjoyed this whole series, but Emery and Rory [from *Scandalous in a Kilt*] have stolen my heart and are now my favorites!"
The Romance Reviews

Other Books by Anna Durand

One Hot Chance (Hot Brits, Book One)

One Hot Roomie (Hot Brits, Book Two)

One Hot Crush (Hot Brits, Book Three)

The Dixon Brothers Trilogy (Hot Brits, Books 1-3)

Natural Passion (Au Naturel Trilogy, Book One)

Natural Impulse (Au Naturel Trilogy, Book Two)

Natural Satisfaction (Au Naturel Trilogy, Book Three)

Dangerous in a Kilt (Hot Scots, Book One)

Wicked in a Kilt (Hot Scots, Book Two)

Scandalous in a Kilt (Hot Scots, Book Three)

The MacTaggart Brothers Trilogy (Hot Scots, Books 1-3)

Gift-Wrapped in a Kilt (Hot Scots, Book Four)

Notorious in a Kilt (Hot Scots, Book Five)

Insatiable in a Kilt (Hot Scots, Book Six)

Lethal in a Kilt (Hot Scots, Book Seven)

Irresistible in a Kilt (Hot Scots, Book Eight)

Devastating in a Kilt (Hot Scots, Book Nine)

Fired Up (standalone romance)

The Mortal Falls (Undercover Elementals, Book One)

The Mortal Fires (Undercover Elementals, Book Two)

The Mortal Tempest (Undercover Elementals, Book Three)

The Janusite Trilogy (Undercover Elementals, Books 1-3)

Obsidian Hunger (Undercover Elementals, Book Four)

Willpower (Psychic Crossroads, Book One)

Intuition (Psychic Crossroads, Book Two)

Kinetic (Psychic Crossroads, Book Three)

Passion Never Dies: The Complete Reborn Series

Reborn to Die (Reborn, Part One)

Reborn to Burn (Reborn, Part Two)

Reborn to Avenge (Reborn, Part Three)

Reborn to Conquer (Reborn, Part Four)

One Hot ESCAPE

Hot Brits, Book Four

ANNA DURAND

JACOBSVILLE BOOKS · MARIETTA, OHIO`

ONE HOT ESCAPE

Copyright © 2020 by Lisa A. Shiel

All rights reserved.

ISBN: 978-1-949406-39-9 (paperback)
ISBN: 978-1-949406-40-5 (ebook)
ISBN: 978-1-949406-41-2 (audiobook)

Manufactured in the United States.

Jacobsville Books
www.JacobsvilleBooks.com

Publisher's Cataloging-in-Publication Data
provided by Five Rainbows Cataloging Services

Names: Durand, Anna.
Title: One hot escape / Anna Durand.
Description: Marietta, OH : Jacobsville Books, 2020. | Series: Hot Brits, bk. 4.
Identifiers: ISBN 978-1-949406-39-9 (paperback) | ISBN 978-1-949406-40-5
   (ebook) | ISBN 978-1-949406-41-2 (audiobook)
Subjects: LCSH: Epidemiologists--Fiction. | Publishers and publishing--Fiction.
   | British--Fiction. | Caribbean Area--Fiction. | Romance fiction. | BISAC:
   FICTION / Romance / Contemporary. | FICTION / Romance / Romantic
   Comedy. | GSAFD: Love stories.
Classification: LCC PS3604.U724 O54 2020 (print) | LCC PS3604.U724 (ebook)
   | DDC 813/.6--dc23.

Chapter One

Maddie

I've found heaven for sure, in this magical place where the sun warms my skin, the azure sky gleams above me, palm trees sway all around me, and toasty golden sand tickles between my toes. After years of bouncing around the globe to pin down the causes of disease outbreaks, I finally have a little time to kick back, exhale, and revel in the freedom to do nothing at all.

Don't get me wrong. I love being an epidemiologist, but I'm so far beyond burned out. My sister, Rika, and her husband booked me a two-week vacation at a swanky Caribbean resort because, she says, I need time off. Since Rika got a sneaky look on her face when she told me that, I think she has ulterior motives. I have no idea what they are, and right now, I don't care.

Even the name of this place seems magical—Elusion Island. When Rika told me the name, I thought she was saying "illusion," which means something that's not real. But she said "elusion," and that word refers to an escape from everyday unpleasantness. Yeah, I need some elusion, big time.

The sun feels wonderful on my skin. I can't remember the last time I sunbathed. I can't remember the last time I wore a bikini either, but Rika had insisted on buying me several of them. Today, I chose a sky blue string bikini that brings out the color of my eyes.

My sister told me so. I haven't ventured into the Caribbean waters yet since I only arrived forty-two minutes ago.

As of right now, I'm no longer counting the minutes, hours, or days. That's what kicking back means, right? Time becomes irrelevant. For two weeks, I'm not an epidemiologist. I'm simply a girl enjoying a tropical escape. I've been lounging on this beach chair for about two minutes, which is a great start to my holiday.

I pick up my mai tai and take a big sip. The cool drink slides down my throat, and I smile at the delicious way the alcohol whispers through me. Slipping on my sunglasses, I lean my head back and close my eyes. *Ahhh…relaxation, I've missed you.* The sultry warmth of the sun soaks into my skin, and every muscle in my body softens. I pull in a long breath and exhale it little by little, letting the sounds and sensations lull me into a drowsy state, floating on a sea of serenity where all the unpleasantness I've experienced evaporates.

No sickness. No death. No overwhelming pressure to succeed. The past drifts away, leaving me with a blessed sense of tranquility.

A shadow drapes over me.

Even with my sunglasses on and my eyes closed, I notice the deeper darkness that's fallen over me and my chair. I open one eye.

A man is standing several feet past the foot of my chair, his shadow spilling over me.

I can't tell if he's looking at me since he's wearing reflective sunglasses. But damn, that man has a killer body. And he's showing it off by wearing nothing but a pair of skintight swim briefs. Tiny ones. Their golden tan color is almost the same shade as the sand. Or is it? My sunglasses have an amber tint, so I can't be positive about that. I lift my shades just enough to see him in the natural light of the sun.

Yep, his swim briefs are the same color as the sand. I let my gaze wander over him, from his face to his broad shoulders and well-defined pecs, then farther down to his impressive abs. His narrow hips guide my attention even lower, to the bulge in his swim shorts and his powerful thighs.

My focus snaps back to his package and stalls there. A new kind of warmth, silky and seductive, shimmers through me. When did I last have sex? I can't remember, and that's just sad.

I force myself to look at his face. His short hair is light brown with gold streaks, possibly from the sun. He looks like he's been here for a while, given his skin has a faint bronzing that makes all his muscles seem even more enticing. I assume that skin tone comes from the sun, or maybe he always looks tanned. I have no idea, but I'd love to find out. Love to explore that body with my hands, my lips, and my tongue.

What on earth am I doing? Drooling over a complete stranger? I never do that. I'm a serious-minded scientist, not a college freshman. But I have gotten so damn tired of being serious and studious and hard-working. This vacation is an escape from my life, so maybe I should let myself really cut loose.

And I'll start by ogling a stranger. A steamy-hot one.

Back to his face…He has rugged features, but they strike me as sexy rather than coarse. His hook nose gives him an aura of manly strength, and I can imagine him skydiving or hunting for relics like Indiana Jones. His lips are full but not too full, just the right amount to make me want to feel those lips on my mouth, my throat, my breasts, anywhere he wants to kiss me.

Wow, I haven't gotten this turned on by a guy in ages. Maybe never. And he hasn't even spoken yet. So yeah, it's clearly been too long since I had sex.

God, I hope he doesn't talk like a surfer dude or have a whiny voice. That would ruin this fantasy I'm dreaming up. It involves him in that swimsuit, free-diving into a cenote in Mexico to dredge up ancient treasures from the depths of a flooded sinkhole.

With my luck, he's a tax accountant who shaves his chest and spray-tans his body.

"Are you done?" the stranger asks, and I detect a British accent hidden in those three syllables.

"Did you want this chair?" I ask. "Because I only just sat down here."

"No, I don't want your chair." His lips, the ones I've been fantasizing about, slide into a sensual smirk. "I wondered if you were done staring at me. Not that I mind. I was staring at you too."

Oh shit. He noticed that? I kind of assumed he'd been admiring the scenery or something. Instead, he'd been admiring me. The realization triggers another wave of sensuous heat that ripples through me. The sexiest man I've ever seen has been ogling me the way I'd done to him.

"Mind if I sit on the sand beside you?" he asks.

"Not at all. It's a public beach."

"Actually, it's a private one for resort guests only."

He saunters closer and settles his taut ass onto the sand, no more than a foot away from my chair.

I take another sip of my drink, in need of the cooling sweetness of the mai tai. Even my cocktail can't diminish the warmth that sizzles over my skin whenever this man speaks or whenever I let my gaze roam over his body. Yeah, I can't stop myself from doing that again. And again. He knew I'd been drooling over him a minute ago, so I doubt he'll care if I do it over and over.

Behind those reflective shades, he might be doing the exact same thing.

The stranger removes his sunglasses, holding them in his hand, and I finally glimpse his sapphire eyes. "Are you here alone? Or do you have a boyfriend or husband or some sort of significant other?"

"No, I'm alone. What about you?"

"On my own too." He glances at my breasts, and his tongue darts out to moisten his lips. "You are the most beautiful woman I've ever seen. That bikini is…incredible."

The rough, hot tone of his voice makes me shiver the tiniest bit. I take my shades off and set them on the little table beside me, where my drink waits. Suddenly, I don't want that mai tai anymore. I'd much rather get intoxicated by the man next to me.

"Your swim briefs are incredible too," I say. Oh God, was that not the dumbest thing I could possibly have blurted out? I'm a medical researcher, which means I have a brain and know how to use it. But this man short-circuits all my common-sense pathways.

"Would you like to go for a walk?" he asks. "Down the beach. It's a lovely day, and I'd be glad for the company."

"Sure. A walk sounds nice."

He rises and offers me his hand.

I settle my palm in his, loving the roughness of his skin, and slip my feet into my sandals. This close to him, I can see he has a dusting of stubble on his face. I love that too. Normally, I prefer clean-shaven men, but the stubble looks so good on this guy. His deep voice makes me want to fan myself, but his body has me lusting for him like crazy. I want to grab my cocktail and guzzle the rest of it. Instead, I let him lead me away from my chair, guiding me down the beach.

We travel farther and farther away from the main section of the beach, the part that's right in front of the resort building. A smattering of palm trees lines the main beach, but now we're moseying into a region with more trees where the palm fronds above shield us from the sun. The occasional rays shower down between the fronds, creating a tranquil atmosphere.

The stranger stops us near a large palm tree. He keeps hold of my hand, turning to face me.

I feel a bizarre need to say something. "My name is—"

"No names. Please." He claims my other hand, so now both of my palms are enclosed in both of his. "I'm leaving tomorrow. Going home. But first, I want to do something I've never done before."

"Like what? I'd love to try parasailing. I hear it's quite an experience."

He draws me closer, placing my hands on his hips, and wraps his arms around me. "I'd love to experience you."

I suck in a breath but can't quite inhale a full one. Did he just suggest what I think he suggested? No, that kind of thing does not happen to me. "What do you mean?"

He pulls me snug against his body. "I want to kiss you, for starters."

For starters? Excitement rushes through me, from my lips that have begun to tingle in anticipation to my toes that wriggle in my sandals like they're urging me to do something as wild as kissing a stranger. What else does he have in mind? I won't find out unless I make a decision.

"I've been drinking a mai tai," I say. "Don't feel impaired, but I thought you should know I had a cocktail."

"You barely drank a few millimeters of what was in that glass."

"That was my first cocktail in a really long time, and the only one I've had today."

"Good." He slides his hands up my back, spreading them over my shoulder blades. "May I kiss you?"

"Yes, please do." Why not? He's hot, and I desperately need to break out of my good-girl routine.

He brushes his lips over mine so delicately, his breaths ghosting over my skin. The feel of his firm body against mine does things to me I haven't experienced in a long time, maybe never. The knowledge that I'm about to be kissed by a total stranger, a man whose name I don't even know, sends an electrifying thrill through me. When he seals his mouth over mine, pressing firmly, I hold my breath and wait, craving so much more than this. He teases me with light flicks of his tongue but still doesn't deepen our kiss.

I moan and sag into him, flattening my palms on his chest, parting my lips and praying he'll give me more.

And he does. He slips his tongue between my lips to explore my mouth with delicate licks and sensuous glides like he wants to map every millimeter of my mouth so he can memorize the contours of it. I whisk my hands up his chest, twining my arms around his neck. He feels amazing, he tastes like everything decadent and forbidden, and the scent of him defies description even while it drives me crazy with the need to do more than kiss him.

His erection is crushed to my belly, skin to skin, like it's broken free from his skintight briefs. I rub myself against that rod, against all of him. My nipples go stiff and ache from the intoxicating way they scrape against his chest through the flimsy fabric of my bikini top.

He groans and peels his mouth away from mine. "I need more of you."

"Oh yes, I want that too."

He feathers his lips over mine, not quite a kiss. "I'm not ready to say goodbye yet. Are you?"

"No, I'm not either."

"I have something I need to take care of first, but I'd love to spend the night with you. Would you come to Room 409 at eight o'clock?"

"Sure."

"Tonight, I'll do better than just a kiss," he murmurs while his lips graze mine. "I want to make love to you all night."

Holy heaven, that sounds amazing. I shouldn't want to do it, but like I discovered earlier when I'd first seen this man, he short-circuits all my common-sense pathways.

"I'd love to do that," I tell him. The rational side of my brain insists I should've told him no, but I don't want to do that. For the first time ever, I'll go for what feels good, no matter how irrational it is. "I'll see you at eight."

He takes my hand and leads me away. We say goodbye on the path that connects the main beach to the resort building, and I go to my room. To flop onto the bed. And stare at the ceiling. No one would believe Dr. Madeleine Solberg is about to have a one-night stand. That's what makes it so exciting.

A smile stretches my lips, then I break into a grin.

Maybe I've lost my mind, but it feels too fantastic to stop now.

Chapter Two

Richard

What am I doing? Not one person who knows me would believe I'd ever concoct an insane plan like the one I proposed to the woman on the beach. She's stunning, and apparently, the sight of her in that skimpy bikini vaporized every last thread of my sanity. Inviting a woman to my room for a night of anonymous sex? The word barmy doesn't even begin to describe my mental state today. But if this is madness, I like it.

That woman…her body…the flavor of her mouth…

Memories of her torment me just as I'm returning from that thing I'd needed to take care of, which turned out to be a fruitless effort. I'd hired a car to drive to a secluded beach where the most reclusive author on earth demanded I meet him. Well, his personal assistant told me to go there. I've talked to Sir Dexter Armstrong-Hill several times on the phone, and I flew to Elusion Island at his request. Now he keeps putting me off. His PA, Ilsa Weingartner, met me at the designated location and gave me the news that Dexter will not see me today.

I'd wanted to persuade a Nobel Prize-winning author to sign with my publishing company, but after a week of failed attempts, I'm done. To hell with the contract. I'm going home.

After I make love to that stunning American woman. I shouldn't be doing this, but I need to do it, for reasons I can't understand. So

I rush out of the elevator the second the doors open and race down the hall to my suite. The clock on my mobile tells me I have four minutes until the sensual beauty I'd met this afternoon will knock on my door. If she turns up. If I don't lose my nerve. That would be preferable to going barmy, but I've already done that. Might as well see this through to the end.

When I shove my keycard into the lock, a light flashes red. I try it again. Red flashes again. My hand is shaking, which is ridiculous, so I have no choice but to stand here for a moment until I've calmed down.

My mobile says it's now seven fifty-eight.

Bollocks. I slide the keycard in more gently.

The light turns green.

I throw the door open, hurry inside, and kick the door shut without even slowing down. I need to change clothes. I've done that twice today already—once when I changed into my swimsuit, and again when I switched to the business suit I'm now wearing—but I don't want to look like a stuffy publisher when that sexy woman arrives.

What if she changed her mind?

Maybe the thought should ease the tension inside me, but it doesn't. I need to see her again, kiss her again, and do so much more than that.

I change into casual clothes and start pacing the width of the room. The sound of the surf reaches me in here, thanks to the open design of this suite, and all the suites at Elusion Island Resort. The regular rooms don't have this design, and I'd wanted the best view possible. One side of the spacious room not only overlooks the bay but is completely open to the outdoors. I stop midway through another circuit of the room and gaze out across the infinity pool, toward the waters of the bay and the horizon beyond it.

The sun has set, and I can barely make out the mountains or the ocean. The lights of the resort cast glistening pools of illumination on the bay.

A knock on the door pulls my attention away from the view.

She's here. The woman actually came.

I straighten my shirt, though it's already straight. Then I walk up to the door and swing it open.

She's standing there. The girl from the beach. Wearing that bikini, along with a sheer white shirt that hangs open and extends past her knees. Her pale-red hair had been tied up in a ponytail earlier, but now it drapes over her shoulders, and curling strands of it kiss her cheeks.

Bloody hell, she looks even sexier and more beautiful now than she did on the beach. I want to kiss her again, as badly as I'd wanted it hours ago. The need is even worse now since I know what her lips feel like and taste like. I remember the softness of her skin too, and the way her eyes turn glossy when she's aroused. I want to see that look in her eyes while I'm inside her.

"Hello," she says, smiling nervously. "I'm here."

"Yes, I know." I move aside and gesture for her to walk into the suite. "Come in, please. I'm glad you're here."

She ambles past me but stops a few meters beyond the doorway. While I shut the door, I watch her head swivel left and right, though I can't see her expression since she's facing away from me. I love the view, though. That long shirt is almost translucent, giving me tantalizing glimpses of every curve on her body. Somehow, it's even more enticing to get a peek at those curves instead of touching them, but I want to do that too. Need to do it. Over and over, all night long.

I've lost my mind, and I don't care.

The woman spins around once, her mouth open and her eyes large. Then she halts facing me and spreads her arms. "I've never seen a suite like this in my entire life. It's…heaven."

She's so adorably stunned that I can't help chuckling. "It's a hotel suite, not a celestial paradise."

"Celestial paradise? Not many people talk that way."

"Sorry. I have a habit of using big words." A side effect of my job, but I don't want to talk about work with her.

"Don't apologize for that," she says. "I use lots of words that are way bigger than the ones you just said. Fancy words are so stimulating."

"Are they? Maybe I should pull up a thesaurus on my mobile so I can seduce you with polysyllabic phrases."

"Ooh, that's hot."

I know she's teasing me, but the longer we speak, the more I want to ravish her. A variety of scenarios for doing that play out in my mind, and I can't decide which one to start with.

"Would you like a drink?" I ask. "There's champagne in the refrigerator."

"Can't remember the last time I had champagne. So yeah, let's have a little of that."

I'd ordered the champagne earlier, along with two glasses, because I hoped this woman would knock on my door. I hurry over to the small refrigerator tucked into the corner, retrieve the bottle and two glasses, and return to her. She's moved to the edge of the infinity pool, gazing out into the deepening night. The first stars are visible, and suddenly I feel like I am in heaven, surrounded by glimmering stars and accompanied by an angel in a blue bikini.

As I stop beside her, I find myself appreciating her profile instead of the night sky.

She turns her face toward me and smiles. "Are you going to pop that cork?"

"Yes, of course." I hand her the two glasses, then struggle to do what she said. The bloody cork won't budge, so I give up. "Afraid I can't get the bottle open. We'll have to skip the champagne."

"Don't worry. I know the trick." She shoves the glasses into my hand and plucks the bottle away from me. With one try, she sends the cork flying into the infinity pool, where it lands with a splash and floats on the surface. "There. Mission accomplished."

Maybe I should feel emasculated by the fact she accomplished a task I'd failed at, but all I feel is more turned on than ever before in my life. If I bought this woman dinner at a posh restaurant, I'm sure she wouldn't order salad with no dressing and pick at it like a bird. She would devour a medium-rare steak with gusto.

And watching her do that would make me want to spread her body across a table in the middle of that restaurant and drive into her.

She pours champagne into the two glasses I'm still grasping, then sets the bottle on the floor. Taking one flute, she holds it near mine. "What should we toast to?"

"Pleasure."

Her tongue sneaks out between her lips, gliding back and forth twice while her eyes get that glossy look. "I like that. To pleasure, then."

We clink our glasses and take our sips.

"Mm," she says, "I love the feel of the fizzy stuff in my mouth, and the way it sizzles down my throat."

I empty my glass in one mouthful. And that "fizzy stuff" bubbles down my throat, making me cough.

The angel in a bikini grins. "You're not supposed to gulp it. Haven't you ever had champagne before?"

"Yes." But not while looking at a woman like her. I don't think there are any other women like her, anyway.

She takes a dainty sip, peering at me over the rim of her glass. "Wouldn't you like to know my name?"

I want that more than she could possibly know, but it's a ruddy awful idea. "That's not necessary. I'm leaving early in the morning, and we'll never see each other again. I'd rather not know too much about you."

"Uh-huh." She taps her fingernail on her glass, studying me with squinted eyes. "I've never slept with a guy without knowing at least his first name."

I lied, of course. I want to know everything about this woman, but getting to know her would only complicate things. My life has no room for dating. Work is all I have time for. And if I know her name, I have a feeling it will be even more difficult to walk away in the morning.

My life has become complicated enough already.

The bikini-clad goddess tosses back her entire glassful of champagne. She shudders, then laughs. "I like drinking bubbly your way. It makes me tingly all over."

Though my mouth opens, I can't speak. Champagne makes her tingly all over? I can see her stiff nipples poking through her bikini top. I love those breasts. I imagine cradling one in my palm and wonder if it will fit perfectly. After the way she shuddered from drinking "bubbly," I want to close my mouth around her nipple and make her shiver for a different reason.

"Enough champagne," I say, snatching her glass away and setting both flutes on the floor. "Where should we shag first?"

"Good thing for you I know what 'shag' means to a Brit, or I might think you're inviting me to install wall-to-wall carpeting for you."

"Carpeting?"

"Yeah. Shag is a type of carpet fiber."

"Oh. Yes, I know." But looking at her scrambles my brain. I should try to unscramble my thoughts, but I don't want to. Responsibility has been my primary concern for as long as I can remember, but it's gotten me precisely nowhere. Successful in business, yes. Well, mostly. Successful in the rest of my life? Not at all. Tonight, with this woman, I want to behave like an unrepentant rake.

I slip an arm under her shirt to encircle her waist, tugging her into my body. "I meant that I want to make love to you, so where should we start? The bed seems awfully prosaic."

She glances around, her bottom lip caught between her teeth. Then she leans into me, spreading her palms over my chest, the warmth of them penetrating my shirt. "Out there. On one of those chairs."

"Where?"

"Right over there, on the patio." She peels one hand away from me to point toward the pair of chaises that occupy the patio. "Out in the open. I've never done anything like that before. Isn't this what tropical vacations are for? Getting wild and dirty? I hope so, because I really want that."

So do I. With her.

"The patio it is," I say, and I strip off my clothes in record time, digging a condom packet out of my trouser pocket. I'd bought a box of those this afternoon too.

My dirty angel pushes the see-through shirt off her shoulders, letting it fall to the floor. She kicks off her sandals. "Would you like to undress me, or should I do it?"

Fuck, I want to strip her naked. To touch her. To taste her.

I slide my arms under hers and take hold of the bow that keeps her bikini top in place. While I untie it, she gazes up at me with a dreamily lustful expression that sends what little blood I have left in my brain rushing down to my cock. I undo the smaller bow that secures the strap behind her neck, and the top flutters down to join her shirt on the floor.

She molds her body to mine, those breasts mounding against my chest. "I want you, mystery man."

And I want her, but my voice has stopped working again. Two more quick movements and I've undone the strings on her bikini bottom, then I grasp the fabric and tear it off her body, tossing it away.

I guide her out onto the patio, stopping near the two chaises.

"Lie down," she says. Then she leans in and purrs, "Please."

How can I resist her? I can't, so I stretch out on the chaise.

The naked goddess kneels over me, straddling my thighs. "Condom?"

I suddenly realize I'm clutching the condom packet in my hand. I'd forgotten I even had the ruddy thing, but I thank heaven I held on to enough of my wits to remember we need protection. I raise the packet. "Here it is. Give me a minute to get it on."

She snatches the packet away and holds it between two fingers, wiggling them at me. "Let me do it for you."

Maybe if she stopped speaking in that sultry voice, I would realize letting her touch my cock is not good for my self-control, but I don't care. She is speaking that way, and she's the sexiest woman in the world. I don't even care that I'm engaging in wild hyperbole.

Taking the packet between her teeth, she tears it open.

I need to fuck her. Right now. Since I can't, because she's kneeling over me, I have no choice but to watch while she pulls the condom out of the foil wrapping and rests her arse on my thighs. The first touch of her fingers on my cock robs me of breath. I struggle to regain it while my pulse accelerates and my erection throbs. She clasps my length, running her hand up and down it twice before she begins to roll the condom over me.

And she takes her time.

Grasping her hips, I follow every movement of her slender fingers with my gaze, transfixed by the sight of them dragging the latex down millimeter by millimeter until she's covered me.

Once she's done, I lunge forward to capture her nipple, licking and suckling it. Her skin tastes salty, but sweet too. How a woman can taste sweet, I have no idea. She does, it drives me mad, and I don't give a toss why.

"Yes," she breathes as she plunges her fingers into my hair to hold me to her breast.

I shove my hands under her arse and urge her to rise onto her knees again. When she does, I keep my hands on those cheeks to drag her forward while I sit back against the chaise, never releasing her nipple. She grips the chair's back, but the part of her I want the most isn't properly positioned yet. I tug her bottom until she shimmies closer. I have to give up the flavor of her breast, but now her mound is in front of my face. *Perfect.*

"You're so beautiful," I say, combing my fingers through the curly hairs that hide the flesh I want to devour. "I need to feast on you and make you come hard and fast, then I plan to bury myself inside your luscious body."

"Please, yes, do anything you want."

I pull her hips closer and shove my head between her legs, sealing my mouth around her taut bud. Her soft gasp drives me even madder, and I push a hand between her folds to stroke her wet flesh while I nip and lap at her nub, rolling my tongue around it. The flavor of her…I can't describe it. But I feel like I've drunk an entire bottle of vodka, too intoxicated to stop now even if I wanted to. I don't want to stop or slow down or think. No more rational thought. I need to make this woman scream.

Her nails dig into my scalp while she clutches my head, panting and moaning and begging me to push her over the edge.

I push a finger inside her.

"Oh God!" she exclaims between sharp gasps.

While I gorge myself on her clit, I slide another finger inside her, then another. I thrust them into her over and over like I'm fucking her—which I am, but not in the way I need to more than anything. Not yet.

She freezes, not even gasping anymore.

I know she's about to come. Desperate to give her that release, I reach up with my free hand to cup her breast and pinch the nipple.

Her body pulses around my fingers, and she screams. Her cries echo off the patio walls. I'm positive other guests must hear it, but nothing else matters except coaxing every last bit of pleasure from her. Once her spasms fade, I pull away from her body, breathing almost as hard as she is.

She bends down to crush her lips to mine, only for a second. "Your turn."

"My what?" I ask, sounding dazed. Well, I bloody am dazed.

The erotic angel impales her body on my cock, throwing her head back to let out a rough, loud groan. "You feel so damn good."

"Ride me, love," I rasp. "Please, do it now before I lose control and, ah, go off prematurely."

I haven't done that since I was a teenager, but no other woman has ever made me feel so…out of control.

She starts moving, slowly at first, then increasing the pace with every rolling thrust of her hips. She's so slick, so hot, and her body wraps around mine like it was designed to fit me and only me. That's complete bollocks, but my lust-addled mind believes it. I love the look on her face—eyes half-closed, lips parted, cheeks flushed—and I love the way she lays her palms on my shoulders while she keeps fucking me. I grasp her hips, urging her to go faster and harder while our bodies generate a wet sucking sound. The climax starts in my spine, barreling downward like a runaway train, the pressure in my cock mounting until I know I won't last more than a few seconds longer.

I shove my fingers between her folds and rub her clit.

Her fingers clench my shoulders hard enough to cause pain, but I hardly notice it. Her head falls forward, bumping my forehead. "Yes, God, yes, I'm about to—"

Every muscle inside her clamps down on my cock, again and again, the pulsating waves pushing me over the edge with her. While she cries out, I erupt inside her, powerless to stop myself from lunging my hips up to penetrate her body so thoroughly that the tip of my cock grazes her inner wall. I come while I'm buried so deep inside her that it's almost like we've merged, and pleasure slams through me, hotter and more intense than anything I've known before.

She collapses against me, her chest heaving, her head on my shoulder.

I've gone limp too, but I marshal just enough strength to wind my arms around her. I'm still nestled inside her body, but I don't have any physical energy left to remedy that. Not that I want to, anyway. She feels so bloody wonderful. We lie there like that for a few minutes, I think. With no clock to tell me the time, I have no idea how long I've cradled this incredible woman in my arms while we both recover from life-altering sex.

Finally, I turn us onto our sides, facing each other, and pull out of her body.

She smiles like a woman who's thoroughly satisfied and relaxed. "That was amazing. Thank you."

"No, thank you. I've never shagged a woman on a patio chaise, and I've never come so hard for any other woman."

"Mm, it was mind-blowing for me too."

I brush sweaty hairs away from her cheek. "Stay with me all night. Please. I need to enjoy your body several more times before I leave for the airport."

"Love to stay." She catches my bottom lip between her teeth and teases it with her tongue, then lets it go. "Can we have more champagne?"

"Absolutely. And I'll order dinner for us." I trace a fingertip down her cheek. "We'll eat in bed."

"Yes, definitely." She sits up and stretches, giving me a lovely view of her tits from underneath. "I need the bathroom first, though."

While she wanders off to do that, I marvel at what's happened to me today. I'd been ready to take a swim, alone, and then embark on my pointless trip to a different beach where Dexter stand me up. After that, I would've hidden in my suite all night. I'm still leaving at six o'clock in the morning. I will never see this woman again. It's for the best since my life leaves no room for a relationship, and besides, no decent woman would want to get entangled in the mess that is my world.

But for tonight, I have a passionate angel in my arms.

That's right, you arse, so enjoy it.

Yes, I mean to do that all night. Who cares about sleeping? I can do that on the plane.

Chapter Three

Maddie

I wake up in the morning alone in an enormous bed, tangled in the sheets. If I'm going to wake up hogtied by Egyptian cotton, I want to feel a hot man lying beside me. But no, I don't get to do that. My mystery man skulked out while I was asleep, though I probably shouldn't characterize it as skulking since he told me he would leave at six o'clock. I tried to stay awake to say goodbye, but my brain had other ideas. It said, "Sleep." So I slept.

The reason I got wiped out involves more than hours of fantastic sex. My companion fell asleep first, so I took the opportunity to, um…snoop. What? He wouldn't tell me his name, and my scientist brain needs to know. I thrive on facts, not cloak-and-dagger stuff. So yeah, I poked around until I found his wallet with his UK driver's license tucked inside it. It looks a lot like an American license, though they format dates a little differently. The license has his photo—and of course, he looks gorgeous in that picture, unlike everyone else in the world who looks like a depressed criminal in a driver's license photo. Well, I look that way, at least.

The most important fact on his license is his name. Last night, I slept with Richard Cornelius Hunter. He lives in someplace called Colchester. I hadn't brought my phone with me to this rendezvous, so I can't google the name of that town to find out where exactly it is. I'll do that once I get back to my room.

Does it even matter now? He's gone. We had mind-blowing sex, I snooped in his wallet, and he sneaked out while I was asleep. End of story. I need to move on and forget about Richard Cornelius Hunter, though I plan to hold the memory of last night in my mind forever. I'm not a sentimental idiot. It's like a mental souvenir, that's all.

I file that memory away in my mind, stretch, and swing my legs over the bed's edge. My soles meet the cool wood floor, and I wiggle my toes to enjoy the sensation. My gaze drifts to the side of the room that's completely open to the outdoors and the fiery glow of the sun rising behind the building where I can't see it. I raise my arms high above my head and stretch again, sighing with contentment. Maybe I should be embarrassed by what I did last night, but all I feel is good. For the first time in ages, I did not think about work for almost an entire day.

Even during the hours between when I met Richard and when we spent the night together, I did not think about my job. I strolled along the beach, enjoyed the scenery, had a fabulous massage in the resort spa, and read a book. Yep, I did that. The workaholic scientist read an entire romance novel in three hours. Sure, it had been a short book. A novella, I guess they call it. Still, I read it in one sitting, taking breaks only to pee and to get a bottle of water. I sat on the resort veranda and read.

That book had been hot, but nowhere near as scorching as last night.

How many times did Richard and I have sex? I lost count. We enjoyed each other in the pool, on the sofa, and finally in bed—twice. We also made inventive use of our mouths and hands to make each other come, so yeah, I can't say for sure how many orgasms were involved. I've never had that much sex in one night. It's left me a little sore, but in a good way. The soreness will be a temporary memento of the best night of my life.

I get up and find my bikini, then put it on and slip the gauzy shirt on over it. Now I'm at least presentable when I walk back to my room on the discount side of the resort building. Richard paid for one of the luxury suites, which makes me wonder if he's rich. Or maybe the company he works for gave him a luxury vacation as thanks for his hard work.

Yeah, right. Employers do that so often.

Maybe his family gave him a Caribbean vacation as a present, but none of that matters because I will never see him again.

I hunt around for a few more minutes until I find my sandals, then I slide my feet into them and head for the door, swinging it open.

A woman with dark, curly hair yelps. She's standing right outside the door holding a keycard in her hand like she was about to open the door herself. Since she's wearing a maid's uniform, I figure this isn't another woman Richard seduced during his stay here.

"Sorry," I say. "Didn't mean to scare you. I was just leaving."

"Don't worry," she says in her lovely Caribbean accent. "I'm used to meeting guests while they're sneaking out of someone else's room."

I don't take offense because she doesn't sound annoyed or disgusted. She sounds like she's had this same experience many times before. And she smiles, which makes me feel less like last night's lover who got caught by the maid.

"Have a good morning," I say while I hurry away.

An hour later, I've changed into jeans and a nice top, with spiffy sandals instead of my beach-appropriate ones. I've also availed myself of the huge breakfast buffet downstairs. Now, I'm back in my room on the second floor trying to figure out what to do for fun today. Sitting on the bed cross-legged, I flip through the mountain of brochures I grabbed from the racks in the lobby and try to decide where to start. Parasailing? I mentioned that to Richard, but the truth is that I have a problem with heights, so it's probably not a great idea. Snorkeling? Yeah, I can handle that. See the fishies, explore a coral reef...

Someone knocks on the door three times.

Maybe it's a maid coming to tidy up my room. I hope it's not the same maid who caught me sneaking out of that luxury suite.

I drop the brochure I've been perusing and climb off the bed. Some of the brochures slide off onto the floor, so I sweep them up in my hands and dump them on the bedspread with the others.

The impatient person outside my door knocks again, three more times.

"Coming," I holler as I race to the door and yank it open.

My heart skips a beat. Seriously, it does. I never thought anybody's heart really did that unless they had an arrhythmia, but mine does. A tingle of excitement sweeps over me from head to toe, awakening every hair on my body.

"Good morning," Richard Cornelius Hunter says.

I gape at him like an idiot. Why is he here? One night only, he said, but now he's standing at my door smiling in his hot British way. Last night, that same smile provoked me to strip naked and practically beg him to do me. Not that I feel like stripping right now. Well, maybe a little bit. He does look thoroughly lickable in khaki pants and a mint green polo shirt. When we met yesterday, he had a shadow beard. When I showed up at his suite, he'd shaved. Today, his morning stubble gives him that mysteriously sexy aura, so yeah, I absolutely do want to tear my clothes off and beg him to fuck me.

But I will *not* do that. No way. A pragmatic researcher does not do things like that.

The me who slept with this guy does not get a say in the matter.

"Are you all right?" he asks. He tugs at his shirt collar. "I shouldn't have come. You don't want to see me again, do you? Of course not. I told you it was a one-off, so—"

"Please stop babbling. It's cute, but you have no reason to be nervous." His nervousness is completely adorable and makes me want to throw my arms around him and kiss him, but statistically, there's no advantage to telling him so. "Why are you here, anyway? Not that I mind. I'm confused is all."

"I, ah…" He hunches his shoulders and gives me an almost shy smile. "I wanted to see you again. You're sweet and sexy, and the hours I spent with you were the best time I've had in years. I'm not ready for it to be over yet. I wondered if you might feel the same way."

"Yes, I do."

"Brilliant!" He almost shouts that word, grinning like a kid who won a giant bag of candy in a raffle. Though I know he's forty, thanks to my snooping, he's not acting like a mature man right now. "May I come in, then?"

"Oh sure, yeah." I move out of the way so he can walk inside the room. "I don't have a mega-suite like yours or the fantastic view you've got, but it's plenty comfy in here."

"I don't care what your room looks like." He glances around. "It's quite nice, actually."

"Thanks." Why am I thanking him like I own this room or something? I didn't decorate it. The niceness of my room is down to the resort owners and the staff who keep it clean and tidy. "Would you like to sit down?"

"Have you eaten breakfast yet?"

"Yeah, I have."

"Oh." He sighs, his shoulders flagging. "I think I will sit down, then."

We settle onto the small sofa—a love seat, really—with no more than six inches between us. He scratches his arm. I bite my lip. He opens his mouth like he wants to say something but shuts it. I tap my fingers on my leg.

"This is silly," I say. "We can talk to each other. We've done that before. It shouldn't be weird just because, um…"

"We had sex all night long?"

"Exactly."

He twists his lip to one side, then the other, while looking everywhere but at me. "Maybe sitting wasn't the right choice."

And he jumps up, shoving his hands in his pockets.

I get up too and set my hands on his chest. "Relax. I'm not about to declare I'm pregnant and demand you marry me. Let's go for a walk or something. If you haven't eaten, we could stop off at the buffet along the way. I wouldn't mind eating a little more papaya."

He aims his sapphire eyes at me. "I want more time with you, that's all. We don't need to have sex again unless you want that. I definitely want it, but I have no expectations."

"I would love to spend more time with you." Rising onto my toes, I wrap my arms around his neck. "Would a kiss be acceptable?"

"Yes, I'd love that."

He loops his arms around me and tugs my body closer. His mouth meets mine, and I can't stop myself from mashing my lips to his. He smells so good, thanks to what I'm sure is cologne or aftershave. The heady scent makes me want him even more, and I imagine him dragging me down onto that tiny sofa so we can screw each other mindless.

But he doesn't even deepen the kiss. When he pulls away, our mouths hover close enough that his lips graze mine.

I've still got my eyes closed, feeling dreamy and floaty and warm. "Mm, Richard."

He stiffens against me. "Why did you call me that?"

I wince and crack my lids open.

The man who made love to me for hours last night is staring at me without blinking, his lips parted.

"You mean why did I call you Richard?" I ask as a pathetic delaying tactic.

"I never told you my name."

"Right." I back away from him and clear my throat. "I, um, kind of snooped around while you were asleep last night. I couldn't stand not knowing your name, it was driving me insane, so I found your wallet and looked at your driver's license."

His gaze narrows, and his mouth crimps.

"I'm sorry," I rush to say. "It was wrong, I know. Never have I ever done anything like that. I've never had a one-nighter either, but I had no call to snoop to find out the name of the guy I slept with. I'm sorry. So, so, so sorry. If you want to leave, I understand."

Richard Cornelius Hunter raises one brow, tilting his head to the side, and studies me for so long that I start to feel warm, though not in a pleasant way.

"Are you okay?" I ask.

Please don't turn into a psycho who's about to chainsaw me into a thousand pieces. Spend the night with an anonymous stranger? It sounded so hot yesterday, but now I'm seeing how stupid I've been. Should I look for something I can make into a weapon? Sure, because I'm MacGyver. *Get a grip, Maddie.*

Richard slings an arm around me, hauls me into his body, and kisses me.

Chapter Four

Richard

*Y*es, I'm kissing her—which must mean I'm barking mad. She tells me she nicked my wallet last night so she could learn my name, and I respond by fastening my mouth to hers. I'm also holding her warm, lush body to mine and relishing the way her breasts are crushed to my chest and the way she smells so bloody incredible, not to mention the way she tastes. I should be irritated by what she did, but instead, I feel aroused. I love that she wanted to know more about me and wanted it so badly that she resorted to espionage.

Maybe she *is* a spy. Or maybe she's just a sexy, nosy American. Either way, her need to know my name makes me want to shag her.

Of course, I have no right to get annoyed. I'm not entirely innocent either, and I experience a sudden impulse to tell her the truth. Peeling her body away from mine, I grasp her upper arms. "I have a confession too, Madeleine."

Her eyes go wide for a second or two, then she shakes her head and curves her kissable lips into a knowing smile. "You snooped on me too. I didn't bring my purse or wallet to your suite, so I'm curious how you obtained that information."

I love the way she talks, using more sophisticated words than most of my clients. They're supposed to be language experts, but too many of them write like twelve-year-olds. Madeleine is clever, for sure, but also elegant. She has an elegantly beautiful body for sure.

"Well?" she says. "Are you going to confess or what?"

"Yes, right." I can't make myself let go of her arms, since I love the feel of her silky skin under my palms. "I bribed the desk clerk to tell me your name. He wouldn't share your last name, though. All I know about you is that your first name is Madeleine, you're American, and you're a bloody brilliant shag."

She laughs, holding a hand to her belly because she's laughing so hard. I think I see a bit of spittle flying from her lips.

I release her arms. "Why is that so funny?"

Madeleine manages to calm herself, though she needs to wipe tears from her eyes. "You did what I did. Here I thought I was the loony one skulking around in the dark to find out who you are, but you did the same thing. It was like our own little two-arm parallel assignment."

What on earth is she on about? Strangely, not understanding a word she said makes me even more aroused. I've probably gone insane, so I should call a psychiatrist immediately. I don't, though. I'm too busy staring at the daft angel standing in front of me. "I have two arms, but I don't understand—"

"A parallel assignment is when multiple groups of participants in a clinical trial each receive different treatments or interventions. A two-arm parallel assignment involves two groups." She points at me and then herself. "You and I are the two arms."

"We're not treating ourselves with drugs." If she's on drugs, that would explain some of her behavior, but I don't believe she's high.

"That was an analogy, and admittedly, not a great one. I say goofy things when I get nervous."

"So do I, apparently. At least when I'm with you."

Madeleine smiles again, and it's so disarming that I want to hug her. "That's so sweet. Thank you, Richard."

"You're thanking me for being nervous around you? That's not the reaction I expected."

She shrugs. "I usually do what everyone expects, but this vacation is my chance to do what I want. Being goofy is one of those things."

"Was sleeping with a stranger on your list of unexpected things to do?"

"Not at first," she says, and her smile becomes wickedly enticing. "But after I met you, yeah, I added that to the list."

"I'm, ah, flattered." Like an idiot, I offer her my hand to shake. "We haven't been formally introduced. I'm—"

"Richard Cornelius Hunter. Yeah, I know, it was on your driver's license." She accepts my hand, folding her fingers around it. "I'm Madeleine Louisa Solberg. The people I like the best call me Maddie."

"And what do the people you don't like call you?"

"Dr. Solberg, mostly."

"I see." I don't, and I want to ask what sort of doctor she is, but first I need to tell her something else. It seems vitally important that I do. "The people I like the best call me Rick."

"May I call you Rick?"

"Please do." I met this woman yesterday and only learned her identity this morning, but I want her to call me Rick. I loved hearing her say "Richard," but I love it even more when she speaks my nickname. "May I call you Maddie?"

"Absolutely. I mean, we had sex last night—lots of sex, in lots of different ways—so I think you've earned the right to call me Maddie."

"I'm glad." I shove my hands into my trouser pockets. "What sort of doctor are you? Sorry. It's none of my business, is it?"

"Sure it is. Why not? I know where you live, down to the street address, so it's only fair I give you a little info about me. I'm an epidemiologist, which means I study diseases and how they spread."

A realization hits me, and I rewind our conversation to a moment ago when she introduced herself. "Did you say your last name is Solberg? One of my mates, Dane Dixon, is married to Rika Solberg. Now she's Rika Dixon, of course."

Maddie flutters her eyelids like she can't believe what she's seeing—or hearing. "You know my little sister?"

"Apparently I do."

"That's an amazing coincidence. Not that I believe in things like that. It's pure chance." She puckers her lips, squinting like she's thinking hard. "Rika encouraged me to take a vacation. She and

Dane paid for this trip and made all the arrangements for me. I remember my sister had wanted to set me up with some guy back before she and Dane got married, but it never worked out. You don't think…"

"They also tried to set me up with a woman, but the timing was never right." I groan as I realize what must have happened. "The Dixons all knew I was coming here to meet with a client. Dane and his brothers encouraged me to extend my visit and make it a holiday. I decided yesterday to cut my stay short, though, and go home. Until I changed my mind about that this morning."

"You've got to be kidding me. Did Dane and Rika arrange this?"

"Well, I doubt they arranged for us to spend the night together, but they certainly organized events so you and I would be at the same resort at the same time."

She throws her head back and growls. "My sister is in so much trouble."

"The Dixon brothers are in trouble too." I rub my jaw, thinking about the situation. "If Dane Dixon and his wife paid for your holiday here, why didn't they get you a luxury suite?"

"They did, but the resort overbooked. Some bigwig got first dibs on the suite I was supposed to have, so I wound up in this room. It's plenty nice."

"I hope you got a refund for the extra cost."

She rolls her eyes. "They gave me vouchers for free spa treatments and stuff."

My stomach chooses this moment to grumble.

Maddie glances at my belly. "We'd better get you some food, huh?"

"Yes, I am very hungry." Though I'd offered to order room service last night, we'd both forgotten about that once the shagging started in earnest. The first time had been incredible, but after her trip to the bathroom, we had abandoned ourselves to the lust. "I owe you a meal. Since you already had breakfast, let me buy you lunch and dinner."

"That's not necessary."

"But I insist." I usher her toward the door. "I'd love to hear more about your job over breakfast."

"Okay. What do you do for a living?"

I pull the door shut and stop. Why do I feel anxious about telling her? Most people think my line of work sounds glamorous, but I'm worried Maddie might think it's tawdry. I'll need to tell her eventually since she told me about her job, so I force myself to say the words. "I own a publishing company in the UK."

"That's amazing." She clasps my hand and starts down the hallway. "I want to hear all about it."

"And I'll tell you—later."

"Sure, whenever. Or don't tell me at all. It's not like we're dating." She casts me a sideways glance. "Are we?"

"Well, I...have no fucking idea."

Maddie laughs. "Me either. We'll figure it out together, hey?"

"Yes, I suppose we will."

I let her lead me onward, to wherever she wants me to go. I'll go anywhere with her. Why? Because she's beautiful, sexy, clever, and fantastic in bed. All good reasons, aren't they? Maybe I'm letting her take me away because I want to shag her again.

Either way, wherever she's taking me, I hope there will at least be food.

Chapter Five

Maddie

I stuff a cupcake into my mouth, tearing off half of it, and moan with a satisfaction deeper than anything I've experienced in years. Well, excluding last night. Not even the best dessert in the world could compare to the way Richard made me feel. Still, I haven't eaten any kind of dessert in a long time. The places I've traveled to usually don't have amenities of any kind, sometimes not even toilets.

So I close my eyes and moan again while I consume the cupcake, then I stuff the other half into my mouth and do it all over again. God, I could almost climax from the satisfaction of consuming a sinfully delicious salted-caramel cupcake with buttery, caramel-y cream cheese frosting. The cake almost melts in my mouth, so silky and luscious, and the frosting delivers that extra boost of creamy decadence.

Swallowing the last crumbs of it, I open my eyes.

Richard's gaze is riveted to my mouth. He has his eyes half-closed while his tongue slides across his bottom lip like he's just eaten a luscious cupcake too.

But he hasn't. My companion chose healthy breakfast choices like fruit cocktail and bran muffins. Honestly, how can a guy who spent all night doing naughty things to me be such a stickler for healthy eating? Sure, I told him I wanted more papaya. But once

I spotted those cupcakes…Healthy dietary choices be damned. I hoped Richard would choose something more fun to eat too, like chocolate chip pancakes with whipped cream and maple syrup. But no, he wanted bran.

Wiping my mouth with a napkin, I notice he's still eying me with a strange expression. "Are you okay? If you want a cupcake, you can have this one."

I offer it to him.

"No, thank you," he says. Then he clears his throat and focuses on his plate, pushing a slice of cantaloupe around on it. "You seemed to be enjoying your cupcake."

"Absolutely. This is a vacation, after all. I'm allowed to indulge in whatever I want."

"You said you weren't hungry."

"I wasn't—until I saw dessert." I half rise from my chair to peer across the dining room toward the buffet tables. One of them is full of cupcakes in various flavors. "They didn't have goodies out earlier. Maybe I'll go try another kind of cupcake. Want one?"

"No. I might have some rice cakes, though."

"Rice cakes?" The second I say that I realize my tone of voice was kind of rude. Sure, I can't believe a man wants to eat rice cakes. It's a thing women force themselves to eat so they can stay slim. But my surprise at his statement is no excuse. I drop back down into my chair. "Sorry. I didn't mean to sound so obnoxious. Your dietary habits are none of my business."

"But you disapprove."

"For all I know, you have food allergies."

"I don't." He carefully cuts off a small piece of cantaloupe and eats it. "But I own a business, which means I have a responsibility to stay healthy and sober."

"Uh-huh. I don't remember champagne being on the food pyramid."

He glances up at me, keeping his head down, and the corner of his mouth slants upward. "It should be."

"You're okay with indulgence when you're trying to get in my pants, but it's taboo the rest of the time."

"I got inside your bikini, not your pants. Though I would love to see you in lace knickers."

"You'd have to get past my pants first."

He lifts his head, those beautiful eyes studying me while his brows crinkle. "How many pairs of knickers do you wear under your trousers?"

"What?" I've spent enough time around the Dixon brothers to know some British terms, like knickers aka panties, but I'm getting the feeling Richard and I are talking about different things right now. "What do you think pants are?"

"Your knickers. What else?"

"Guess you haven't slept with an American before, huh? To us, pants are…" I lift my leg to the side, showing him my jeans, and I point at them. "Pants. The things that cover my legs so I don't get arrested for public indecency. These are jeans, but also pants. As in…pants."

"Oh," he says, drawing out the syllable like he's suddenly grasped my meaning. He smiles and chuckles. "In my country, pants are underwear."

"You Brits sure are strange."

"But don't Americans talk about underpants?"

"Sure, but we don't call them just 'pants.' That would be weird."

"Instead, you lot call your undergarments 'underpants' and also call your trousers 'pants.' No, that's not confusing at all."

He's grinning now, and I love that expression. He looks even sexier when he grins, and so full of joy that it lights him up. It lights me up too. We're not even naked, yet it's the second-best time I've had in way too long. The first-best would be last night, of course.

I get up and sidle around the table to his side, leaning in to whisper in his ear. "You really should try indulging yourself. You rocked at that last night. Sinking your teeth into a soft, succulent cupcake feels almost as good as sex."

He turns his head, our faces now an inch apart. "I'll have one of every flavor of cupcake. Then I'll need to take you back to my suite and fuck you for at least an hour."

"Working off those calories with you will be lots more fun than exercising in the gym."

"I agree." He flicks his tongue out to taste my lips. "That does taste delicious, but it's not as succulent as you."

Heat flashes through me, from my face down to my toes, and especially between my thighs. My voice sounds huskier when I tell him the naked truth. "I want to crawl under the table, unzip your pants, and take you in my mouth so I can indulge in the feel and flavor of your cock."

"We're in a room full of people."

"I know. And I still want to make you come in my mouth."

"Go on and do it."

I want to do it. Damn, do I want to. Never have I gone down on a man anywhere except in the bedroom. But for this man, I really would crawl under the table and take him in my mouth.

But I can't. That annoying good-girl voice in my head says it's wrong. I've been here for less than twenty-four hours, but maybe in a few more days, I'll overcome my inhibitions and do what I suggested.

I straighten. "I'll get those cupcakes."

"Choose whichever ones appeal to you. I'll try some too."

"Good."

I start to walk away, but he captures my wrist in his hand to stop me.

"Could we get those cupcakes in a takeaway box?" he asks. "I'd like to show you a place I found nearby."

"A secret place, I hope. That would be hot."

"Not sure if anyone else knows about it." He skims his thumb over the sensitive skin on my palm. "I'd much rather try those cupcakes when we're completely alone."

I love the sound of that. The good girl in me, who I call Dr. Solberg, is about to faint. But Maddie, the me who's sick of behaving, is clamoring to get out.

Maddie wins.

"Sure," I say. "I'd love that."

"Brilliant." He stands, and his body is so close to mine that I can smell his aftershave and feel his clothes brushing against my skin. "I need to get something from my room. Meet me in the lobby in ten minutes, and wear walking shoes."

He leans in like he's about to smack one on me, then seems to realize where we are—in the dining room with tons of people around—so he kisses my cheek instead.

I watch him leave the dining room, and I wonder.
Who is Richard Hunter?

Chapter Six

Richard

Maddie and I reconvene in the lobby and head outside, aiming for the dirt trail labeled "nature preserve" with a large green arrow pointing down the path. I'm carrying a satchel over my shoulder with the takeaway box full of cupcakes inside it, along with water bottles, paper napkins, and a blanket. I move my hand toward hers, wanting to clasp it, but pull it away. Maybe she won't want me holding her hand. Or will she be offended if I don't? It's hard to know these days. I've been soundly slapped a couple of times when I tried to take a woman's hand. But others get testy if I don't do it.

Sometimes I wish I lived in medieval times. Sure, men sometimes acted like arseholes and forced women to marry them, but at least they never needed to worry about sexual misconduct charges.

Maddie notices it when I stop short of holding her hand—and she clasps mine.

We walk down the trail hand in hand, discussing the scenery and the amenities at the resort. We stay away from personal topics and work-related subjects, though I'm not sure why. Maybe because I told her I don't know if we're dating, and she's not sure if that means I don't want to talk about my life, personal or professional. I don't *want* to talk about that, but I'll have to eventually. I feel a strong need to know everything about her, and satisfying my curiosity will mean I also have to explain parts of my life that aren't terribly pleasant to discuss.

This leaves me with one option. I don't ask her any questions. At least, none more intrusive than when I say, "How do you like the resort so far?"

"It's beautiful." She smiles and shrugs. "But I've only been here since yesterday afternoon, so I can't offer a definitive assessment."

Her smile is so lovely that I want to kiss her, but she starts talking about the flowers and the trees, and I don't get the chance to taste her lips again. Not yet.

As we wander farther down the dirt path, the forest gradually thickens around us, and the branches form a canopy above our heads with the sunlight trickling through the gaps. It dapples Maddie's face with shadow and light, lending her a mysterious air and making her eyes seem darker, though no less beautiful. When I guide her off the prepared trail, traveling down a narrow and grassy but well-worn path, she raises her brows.

"Where are we going?" she asks. Pointing behind us toward the dirt trail, she adds, "It looks like the nature preserve is that way."

"The official trail is back there, but we are inside the preserve now. I'm taking you to a secret place I found a few days ago."

"Are you taking me to your clandestine sex cave so you can do wicked things to me?"

"I've already done that several times over, without the cave."

Yes, I want to ravish her again. And again. And again. But mostly, I want to show her the spot I found, one that's not on any map of the resort or the preserve. I want to share it with her because being with Maddie makes me feel completely relaxed for the first time in years.

We emerge from the shelter of the trees and walk into a small clearing where the sun shines down on us from a clear blue sky, the color so intense that it reminds me of Maddie's eyes. Not a single cloud mars the sky. In front of us, a gentle waterfall spills over a cliff into a small pool, stirring up foam. A grassy ledge surrounds the pool and ducks behind the cascade, while the mist rising from it creates a ghost of a rainbow.

"This is it," I tell Maddie, setting down my satchel.

"It's amazing," she says, releasing my hand to turn in a circle, her head tipped back. "Thank you for bringing me here, Richard."

"Can I convince you to call me Rick? I've already said you can."

"Okay, I will. Rick." She licks her lips, then runs her tongue along the bottoms of her top teeth. "I like the way that slides over my tongue. It's always been one of my favorite names because it's so damn sexy. Rick. Mm, I could say that all day and all night. Rick."

She turns the solitary syllable into a throaty, erotic tease.

All I can do is stare at her. I've never met a doctor who behaves the way she does.

"Gotta say that again," she announces. "Ri—"

I silence her with two fingers on her lips. "Don't say my name like that again unless you want me to do things to you that will disturb the local wildlife."

She laughs, though my fingers muffle it, and mumbles something.

I remove my fingers. "Sorry, I couldn't understand that."

"What I said was that it would be worth triggering a stampede of wildlife if you're making me scream for the right reasons." She presses her body against me, her mouth a hair's breadth from my lips. "Being around you turns me into a nymphomaniac."

"Whatever the male version of a nymphomaniac is, you're turning me into that."

The clothes she's wearing ensure that I desperately want to shag her. She changed while I was getting what I needed from my room, and now she's wearing a flower-pattern bikini top with shorts that barely cover her arse and a sky blue blouse that hangs open. Her walking shoes are sky blue to match her shirt. In that outfit, she looks so entirely fuckable that I can't think about anything except all the ways I plan to make her scream my name just like she suggested.

But not out here. She deserves a soft mattress under her, not dirt and weeds that will get stuck in places no one wants them.

Though I stop myself from undressing her, I can't prevent my lips from finding hers or my tongue from thrusting inside her mouth. She tastes faintly of caramel cupcakes, but when I plunge deeper, all I taste is her—a flavor I can't describe because no words in any language will suffice. She slides her tongue around mine and moans, the sound rife with intense pleasure and hunger.

I could kiss her all day.

She writhes against me, her body rubbing on my cock. "Let's go for a dip in the waterfall."

"That sounds wonderful, but I didn't bring my swimsuit."

"You can swim in your underwear." She tugs the waistband of my trousers and peeks inside them. Head down, she glances up at me. "You seem to have forgotten your pants, Rick."

I think she enjoys calling me Rick strictly because she knows how randy I get when she speaks my name in that seductive tone. "I avoid wearing pants as much as possible. They're bloody annoying. By the way, I love that you're using the British word."

"Just showing a little respect for your culture. Though I think other words are sexier—like briefs or boxers."

"Maybe I prefer thongs."

She skates her hands up my chest, shaking her head. "Men who wear polo shirts don't buy underwear that's made for gigolos."

"But women who are epidemiologists do wear string bikinis."

"Guess you think being a medical researcher means I should be an uptight geek who wears duct-taped eyeglasses."

"I've never met a medical researcher before, so you're the only example I have." I palm her arse with both hands. "Please forgive me. What can I do to make up for that egregious insult?"

"Feed me cupcakes."

Well, at least we both use the same word for those.

I spread the blanket out on the ground beside the satchel and bring out the food and water bottles. "Sit down, please."

She does that, but then stretches out on the blanket on her back.

"That's not sitting, Maddie. Or do Americans have a different word for that?"

"Don't you want to shag me on the blanket?"

"I'd love to, but I was hoping we could do something less exciting right now."

"Like what?"

Her body, in that bikini and spread out on that blanket, looks so tantalizing. I want her, but after the many times I enjoyed her body last night, I shouldn't touch her. What if she's sore? She hasn't acted like she is, but it might take a while before the soreness sets in.

Scratching my jaw, I force myself to focus on her face. "I'd like us to talk. Get to know each other. Is that all right?"

"I thought you had to go home."

"Well, I told you I changed my mind about that." I kneel on the blanket beside her. "I had planned to stay here for two weeks, but after one week I was sick of it. Until I saw you on the beach. That blue bikini changed my mind."

"I'm glad you're here. Taking a solo vacation sounded like fun until I got here. Sitting on the beach drinking a mai tai by myself kind of sucks. Having a friend to talk to is nice."

"Are we friends? So far, all we've really done is shag."

"We're becoming friends." She sits up. "I'm still confused. You said you were leaving, so how did you keep your suite?"

"I had checked out, but halfway to the airport, I told the taxi driver to bring me back here. The suite was still available since I'd booked it for two weeks."

"Glad you came back." She stretches her lithe body and sighs. "I could get addicted to shagging you. And I think I'll keep using that word. It's cute."

"Do you think the word fuck is cute too?"

She rolls her eyes. "Fuck is hot, not cute. But the word shag is just adorable."

"When my mate Chance told me that American women think 'shag' is cute, I assumed he was misinformed. I think the only American women he ever dated were his ex-wife and his current wife."

"Nope, it's true. Just ask my sister."

"I'll take your word for it." I drag my satchel closer and bring out the box of cupcakes. "Now, let's have a snack."

She grins and rubs her hands together.

Maddie might think the word shag is adorable, but not even the cupcakes I'm holding could be sweeter or more enticing than the woman before me. I could get addicted too—to her body, her smile, the barmy things she says, and especially her uninhibited ways.

To hell with work. I'm officially on holiday.

Chapter Seven

Maddie

Richard and I enjoy the cupcakes for a while without talking, though we do feed each other. He holds one to my mouth, but when I open up to take a bite, he shoves the entire thing in there. Frosting gets smeared all over my mouth and on my cheeks too. I get my revenge by stuffing a cupcake into his mouth and purposely smearing it all over him. Then I lick the frosting and crumbs off his skin, taking my sweet time doing that because I love how turned on it gets him.

We both had said we wanted to get to know each other, but we're having too much fun with food to do much talking. We laugh a lot. And we do take a dip in the pool under the waterfall. I wore a bikini, so I'm pretty much ready to go. All I need to do is ditch my shorts and shirt, then jump in. Richard is still deciding whether to keep his khakis on while I practice my butterfly stroke. I've never been good at that, and I haven't gone swimming in a long time, so I give up and just paddle around.

Finally, Richard strips naked and joins me.

We do nothing more titillating than splashing each other, but we still have a blast.

By the time we walk back to the resort, it's lunchtime.

Rick and I change into swimsuits and get our meals to go, then find a secluded section of the beach where we can relax under an umbrella of palm trees while we eat and talk.

"Since you've seen my driving license," he says, "you know how old I am. I don't normally ask women their ages, but it seems only fair that I get to know yours."

"I agree. It's fair." I pop a grape into my mouth and chew it slowly before answering. "I'm thirty-two."

His lips tighten into a teasing smile. "That old? You seem much younger."

"Well, I am younger—than you. Eight years younger, to be precise." I pick up another grape and roll it between my thumb and forefinger. "I like precision. It's a side effect of my job."

Why am I saying the most boring thing imaginable? My need for precision and my obsession with gathering data won't make him hot for me. And ever since I met Richard Hunter, I've developed a new obsession—shagging him.

Oh yeah, that's my new favorite word.

"You mentioned you're an epidemiologist," he says. "I don't quite know what that is."

Nobody does. Even once I explain, most people still have that baffled look on their faces.

I lean back against the palm tree behind me. "I'm a disease detective. That's the common term for it. It's not a sexy job. Basically, I do lots of research, gather data, collate statistics, look for patterns. Whenever there's an outbreak of a new disease or an old one, epidemiologists like me show up to ferret out the source and come up with a treatment. Until ten days ago, I was in Ethiopia working with my colleagues to pinpoint the source of an Ebola outbreak."

"Did you succeed?"

"Yes. But a dozen people died before we got there. Eight more died after we showed up." My throat goes dry, and though I try not to, I remember the sight of those bodies lying under white sheets. "The site was way out in the boonies, and nobody could get the right medicine to the village until we brought the stuff. The treatments don't always work, though."

"Do you work for a hospital or an organization or something?"

I grab my half-eaten sandwich, my gaze aimed at the food while I try to shake off the memories. "I used to be with Doctors Without Borders. After that, I took jobs with various organizations, wherever I was needed."

"That all sounds past tense."

"Because it is. I'm unemployed or taking a sabbatical, whatever you want to call it. Though I have been offered a job at the CDC, which is the Centers for Disease Control. It's in Atlanta, Georgia." I drop my sandwich and reach for the bottle of beer I've been nursing while we eat, then I take a large swig of it. Naveen Misra recommended me for the CDC position, but I haven't decided if I want to work with my ex. Or if I want to be a disease detective anymore. "I got burned out, I guess. A human being can only watch so much suffering before it starts to eat away at your soul. Or maybe it's just me. Maybe nobody else feels that way. I needed to get away from my job and my life for a while so I can decide what I want to do moving forward."

"I understand how you feel," he says. "My career has become a sort of albatross around my neck. Partly my fault. I made a few questionable decisions that have congealed into one massive pile of shit, and I'm trapped underneath the whole stinking mess."

I lean toward him, sniffing. "I don't smell any shit."

"When I said it's a 'stinking' mess, I meant that as a metaphor."

"Yeah, I know. Just trying to make you smile, but I failed." I couldn't even make myself smile. We both need a cuddle, I decide, so I wriggle sideways to edge closer to him and rest my head on his shoulder. "I'd like to hear more about your work, if you want to tell me."

"Later." He grabs his beer bottle and guzzles the remaining half of it in one long gulp.

He's reluctant to talk about himself. I get that. I mean, I'm not exactly thrilled to discuss my life either.

"Let's talk about you some more," he says. "Where did you go to medical school?"

"Nowhere. I'm not a physician."

"But you're an epidemiologist, and you said people call you Dr. Solberg. Your sister tells everyone you are a doctor."

Oh, Rika. I know she means well, but really, she has a bad habit of giving people the wrong impression of me.

"I love my sister," I tell Richard, "but she tends to exaggerate when she's talking about me. Well, it's more like she lets other people infer the wrong conclusion from what she says. I'm not an MD. I have a PhD, a doctorate in epidemiology."

"Your sister says you're her hero because you save lives every day."

"Let me guess. Rika has everyone believing I'm a superhero doctor who cures people with a wave of my hand." I drink some beer before I say more. "I'm afraid it's nothing that glamorous or exciting. It's mostly a numbers game for me. Once I've collated and analyzed all the data, I work with my colleagues to come up with a treatment for the disease in question. I also look for ways to prevent another outbreak. Finding out where an outbreak started is key, but I'm not a cop who arrests the bad guys. And I don't directly save lives like surgeons do."

"But your work is critical. You shouldn't downplay the importance of what you do."

"I don't. Maybe I'm uncomfortable with how my sister has been describing me to other people when I'm not around, but I'm proud of the work I've done."

"As you should be."

I sneak an arm behind him to loop it around his waist. "Now, are you going to share your burnout story with me, or do I have to torture it out of you?"

"I don't have a good reason for my burnout. You're exhausted from traveling the world to help people. I've just…published books."

"Come on, that's nothing but an excuse for not opening up." I hook my leg over his and tickle his ear with my lips. "Guess it's torture, then. The steamy kind that'll make you explode."

"All right, I surrender. I'll tell you my story."

Chapter Eight

Richard

Maddie is one hundred percent right, of course. I despise talking about myself, and I especially don't like admitting I'm knackered from years of working sixteen-hour days while trying to appease prima donnas and outright arseholes. Not all my clients are awful, but the few who are have made my life hell.

But Maddie has a point. I'm avoiding the inevitable. If I want to get to know her, I need to explain my life.

With a sigh, I resign myself to confessing. "My father started a publishing company before I was born. By the time I turned fifteen, Hunter Publishing had become one of the most successful small publishers in the UK. Five years after that, the company had gained international renown for producing some of the best nonfiction books on the market and for its growing list of bestsellers. Once Dad decided to branch out into fiction, the business took off."

"That's amazing. When did you start working there?"

"After university, I took a job as an intern at Hunter Publishing. My father insisted on it. He told me I needed to learn every aspect of the business and work my way up to taking over for him." I lay a hand on her thigh, where it drapes over mine, and use caressing her soft skin as an excuse not to speak for a moment. Or maybe I do that strictly because I love touching her. "When I was thirty-four, my father handed the company over to me. I wanted to make him proud, but instead, I ran it into the ground."

"What happened?"

I shrug one shoulder. With Maddie tucked against me, I can't shrug them both. "I was trying to bring the company into the twenty-first century. Dad liked to keep things as they were, as they'd always been. I had grand ideas about modernizing and attracting younger authors who might bring us a new audience to complement our existing customer base. So I courted a few celebrities."

Maddie wriggles her toes, tickling my leg. "Sounds exciting."

"Not really. Not for me. I've never thought of fame as being a great accomplishment in itself."

"True. But you were trying to promote your company, right?" She pokes me in the side, gently. "Come on, you have to tell me the rest."

"First, I signed an Olympic sprinter, Helmut Beyer. He had suffered an injury that nearly destroyed his career but came back from it to win the gold medal. Helmut also broke the world record for the most social media followers for an athlete."

"Sure, I remember that guy. He got on all the talk shows."

I watch the waves lapping against the shore for a few seconds before I summon the nerve to tell her the rest. "I paid Helmut a rather large advance, but the book was a smashing failure."

"Doesn't 'smashing' means something was really good? But you called it a failure."

"I was being ironic." I wince when I remember the outcome of my next attempt to bring my company into the new millennium. "After that, you'd think I would have learned my lesson about celebrities. But I didn't. I signed a reality TV star who had a massive fanbase. I suppose I assumed the Helmut Beyer disaster was a fluke, and that Danisha Davies would be different."

"But something went wrong."

"Her book was a number-one bestseller in the UK and the US, and the profits poured into Hunter Publishing."

Maddie smiles. "You saved the company."

Her smile makes me feel...completely undeserving of her praise.

She tips her head to the side, studying me. "Why do you say you ran your company into the ground? You had one flop, followed by a big success."

I laugh without any humor. "Yes, it sounds brilliant, doesn't it?"

"Why do you say that like it's not true?"

"Because it isn't." I rub my eyes and sigh. "I'm an idiot and an arse."

"You're neither one."

"Which you know after spending twenty-four hours with me."

"I'm a good judge of character." She nuzzles my cheek. "There's clearly more to the story, so tell me the rest."

"Three days before I left for the Caribbean, I found out Danisha Davies had plagiarized her entire book. She stole the unpublished memoirs of another, lesser-known reality star who had been good friends with her."

"But you didn't know what Danisha had done."

"Doesn't matter." I cover my face with my palms, groaning again, then I lower my hands. "The other woman, Miriam Watkins, is suing Danisha Davies and Hunter Publishing for copyright infringement. This could destroy the company."

"How is it your fault she plagiarized stuff? If it was from an unpublished memoir, you had no way of knowing."

"We have a contract with Danisha, which means we are responsible for ensuring everything we publish meets all legal requirements. Every contract includes an indemnification clause, but she's claiming we committed secondary infringement because she told us where she got the material and we went along with it. We didn't do that, but she has forged emails that make it look like we're complicit."

"I hope you're fighting it."

"We're trying. But the legal costs involved in disproving her claims could be steep, and we can't be sure of a favorable judgment in court." My head falls back against the palm tree like it's become so heavy that my neck can't hold it up anymore. "The day I left for the Caribbean, our solicitors informed me that we should settle with Miriam Watkins and agree to her demands, which include monetary damages. For legal reasons, I can't share all the details. I started the process of removing the book from sale, but the lawsuit coupled with the failure of Helmut Beyer's book might bankrupt the company unless I inject my own money into the settlement deal. So yes, I have run my company into the ground. My father's legacy is in tatters, and I am a disgrace."

Chapter Nine

Maddie

"You are not a disgrace," I say. "Nobody could've guessed that author would turn out to be a plagiarist and a liar. I'm sure your dad will understand if you explain what happened. Have you told him yet? If not, you really should. Wondering how people will react is torture, so stop doing that to yourself and just talk to him."

He screws up his mouth but then sighs and bows his head. "I know you're right. I've known it since the day I found out what Danisha Davies had done, but I'm too much of a coward to tell my father. Then I'll have to inform the board of directors, and who knows what they'll do. My company's reputation will be destroyed, and I will probably be sacked."

"Will you be bankrupted, personally, if you use your money to pay the settlement?"

Rick twists his mouth up again, his face pinched. "No, I'll be all right. Not as well off as before, but hardly penniless. The scandal alone could destroy the company, though."

"I'm so sorry you're going through all of this."

"Don't feel sorry for me." He turns his eyes to look at me, his head still bowed. "I'm sure you've experienced much worse things."

"It's not a competition. But yeah, I've watched people die and been helpless to stop it. That's part of the reason I'm so burned out. After my last assignment, I felt emotionally wrung out and raw." I don't want to remember those events, but my mind disobeys my command and shows me a replay of the worst moments. "It's horrible to watch adults wither away, but it's the children who really tear your heart out. I cried every time a child succumbed. Ebola can be up to fifty percent fatal, which means there isn't much we can do. I still have nightmares about it."

He slings an arm around my shoulders and pulls me close. "I wish I could do something to make you feel better. No one deserves a stress-free holiday more than you do."

"We both deserve that."

"May I ask a personal question?"

"Sure."

Rick hesitates for a moment, twining a lock of my hair around his finger, then letting it unravel. "Why don't you have a boyfriend or husband?"

"I've dated. Until a couple of months ago, I was involved with a virologist I met in Somalia last year. It didn't work out, though. We both work too much to keep a relationship going."

"Yes, I've had the same problem. Working sixteen-hour days might keep my company afloat, but it doesn't leave time for relationships." He braces his chin on top of my head. "I never married either. Most days, I eat al desko."

"Do you mean alfresco?"

"No, al desko. It's a British term that means I eat at my desk, alone."

"Yeah, me too."

He strokes my arm, gazing out across the serene blue waters of the Caribbean Sea. For a few minutes, we don't speak. He holds me, and I rest my cheek on his shoulder. I met this man yesterday, but somehow, he knows exactly what I need and when I need it. I can't believe I told him so much about myself, but he shared a lot of himself too. How can I feel an intimate connection with a virtual stranger?

Maybe I should stop worrying and let myself enjoy this.

"I have an idea," he says.

"Love to hear it."

"We should spend the next two weeks together, doing anything and everything that's fun and frivolous. No talk of work. No more serious conversations. We enjoy each other's company, that's all, and then we say goodbye if that's what we want. No strings, except on your bikini."

"I'd love a two-week escape from real life."

"So would I. Should we do it, then?"

"Absolutely."

He kisses the top of my head. "Wonderful. Let's start right now, by taking a walk down the beach."

"Sounds perfect."

Richard gets up, picking me up with him, and sets my feet on the sand. Hand in hand, we stroll down the shore with crystal-clear blue water on one side and swaying palm trees on the other. I'd kicked off my shoes and left them on our blanket, so I revel in the warmth of the sand slipping between my toes and sliding along my soles.

He keeps watching me—or rather, glancing at my belly region. Lower belly. Maybe he's staring at my hips. Whatever's caught his attention, it's kind of weird.

Suddenly, he stops us and turns toward me. "Christ, I'm an arse."

"What? Not sure where that comment came from. You're a complete gentleman."

"No, I am not." He nods toward my lower body. "You keep wincing and touching your hip like it hurts. But it's not your hip, is it? I ravaged you for hours last night. You're sore."

Okay, yeah, I am. It's not awful, though, and I'm no wimp when it comes to pain. But the stricken look on his face proves to me that he thinks he's damaged me severely.

I spread a palm over his cheek. "Relax, I'm okay. Sure, that was more sex than I've had in a long time, maybe ever, but I'm only a little sore. I'll be fine, promise."

"But I should have known better than to…abuse your body that way."

"There was no abusing. I could've said no after the second time, or the third time, but I loved being with you. A little soreness is worth it."

He rubs the back of his neck, veering his gaze away from mine. "Maybe you aren't horribly sore, but I still think we shouldn't have sex again for a while."

"I'll be good to go tomorrow."

"I believe you, but let's try not shagging for a few days at least, maybe even a week. We can take this time to enjoy each other's company without the distraction of sex." His lips twitch into a slight smirk. "I may need a blindfold to accomplish that, though. Your body is the most distracting thing I've ever seen—or felt."

"Would you rather I wear baggy pants and bulky sweaters?"

"No." He starts walking again, still holding my hand. "I'll manage in spite of your distractingly gorgeous body."

"Not sure I can restrain myself if you're wearing skintight swim briefs." I'm not joking. His bod in that swimsuit…Damn, it's like the scent of fresh donuts wafting out of a bakery down the street. I want to run there, grab all the donuts, and gorge myself on them. His "donut" is hidden inside a single layer of spandex. And yes, I want to pull it out and feast on him. Which gives me an idea. "During our escape-from-real-life thing, is oral sex allowed?"

He chuckles. "Determined, aren't you? I can't be so amazing in bed that the thought of doing without gives you withdrawal symptoms."

"Just trying to make sure we have the best possible time for the next two weeks."

"Let's try not talking about sex for at least an hour. See how it goes."

"All right, if you insist." I bump into him on purpose and give him a teasing smile. "But you're the insatiable beast who seduced me over and over."

"I know, but I'm giving this my best effort." He lets go of my hand, draping his arm around me. "How about a swim? The cool water might ease your soreness."

"What a fantastic idea. Skinny dipping?"

"Didn't you hear what I said about your body? I won't survive two minutes with you naked in the water."

"My bikini is skimpy. I'm practically naked already."

His gaze wanders down my body. "Let's keep up the illusion that you're not naked. For my sake."

"Okay." I give him a quick kiss. "Guess my willpower is stronger than yours."

"I'll order a gold medal for you."

He picks me up and races into the water up to his knees, then he tosses me in.

I shriek while water splashes up around me and I sink beneath the gentle waves. When I surface, I'm completely soaked. "Oh, you'll pay for that, Rick."

"Looking forward to it." He belly-flops into the water, spraying it over me. Shaking his drenched head, he grins. "Let's race to that rock over there."

He points toward a boulder that sits half-submerged maybe fifty feet from the shore.

"You're on," I say, and I start swimming.

Every time I think I've got him pegged, Richard Hunter reveals another hidden facet to his personality. The sensual lover, the sweetheart who came back for me, the businessman who fears he'll lose his company, the caring man who worries about making me sore, and now the playful Brit who wants to swim with me.

We race to the boulder, and I get there first. Hoisting myself up onto the rock, I cheer Richard on while he catches up to me. We're both breathing hard, yet I feel exhilarated.

"You cheated," he says. "Took off before I could get started."

"We can do it again, and I'll let you win this time."

"My ego isn't that fragile." He plants his hands on the rock and levers himself out of the water, holding his body in that position. "You've earned a prize. I don't have a medal for you, so I'll improvise."

He covers my mouth with his own, sliding his tongue between my lips, teasing me with light flicks until I moan and my body slackens. He glides his tongue around mine and sucks on the tip. Then he pulls away, though he's still propped up with his powerful arms, his biceps bulging from the effort.

Flashing me a sexy smile, he dives back into the water.

And I dive in too, swimming in his wake all the way back to the shore. We sprawl on the sand, half in the water, and lie there while we catch our breath. The sky stretches out above us in every direction, a blanket of unblemished blue, and the waves lap against our bodies like a thousand butterfly kisses on our skin. So what if I'm jumbling up my metaphors? This moment feels so…perfect.

I've never believed in love at first sight. Still don't. But this guy makes me consider the answer to a question I never dreamed I'd ask myself. Could I fall for a guy in two weeks?

Guess I'm about to find out.

Chapter Ten

Richard

Madeleine Solberg is the most incredible woman on earth. Hyperbole has never been a weakness of mine, but she makes me want to spout overblown statements every five seconds. When I tossed her into the water, she screamed and grinned. It was the most beautiful thing I've ever seen. But I seem to say that a lot since I met Maddie. Everything she does is the most wonderful, everything she says is the most enchanting, and everything about her is the most alluring.

What's happening to me? I don't care. If anyone tries to explain it to me, I will seal their mouths with the strongest tape available. I don't want to hear how barmy this is, taking up with a woman I've just met and shagging her so many times that I've made her sore. I loved taking her body again and again, but no one would believe I'm capable of sleeping with a stranger, much less spending two weeks in the Caribbean without thinking about work. But that's what I want to do.

The solicitors need time to sort the lawsuit nonsense and find common ground for a settlement, which means my company will survive until I get home. After that, I don't know. What I do know is that I might have a nervous breakdown if I don't relax.

Something about Maddie inspires me to behave like a randy college boy. That's appropriate, though, isn't it? We're about to embark on a frivolous holiday, after all.

And it feels fucking fantastic.

For the rest of the day, we explore the nature preserve—and somehow, I restrain myself and do not ravage her body. I've stopped counting minutes and hours. I left my watch in my suite, and I don't look at the clock on my mobile. I kept it with me in case of emergency. Never know, a flock of parrots might assault us in a tropical version of that Hitchcock film. After a good while of strolling through the wilderness, we take a break to sit beside a stream while birds I've never seen before sing lovely songs all around us.

Before we left the resort, Maddie had exchanged her jeans and blouse for a bikini and skimpy shorts, and she tied her hair up in a ponytail. Before that, she'd swapped her ensemble from last night for the jeans. How many times will she switch her outfits today? Not that I mind. She does look beautiful in her shorts and bikini and as edible as ever. Still, I find myself admiring her face instead of her breasts and thinking about how much I love holding her in my arms rather than the things I'd love to do to her naked body. I don't know what it means, the fact I'm thinking up bad poetry about her eyes instead of seducing her. I don't care. For two weeks, I'm ordering myself to stop thinking.

That's right. No more thoughts. I'll be a brainless idiot, but at least I'll have a bloody good time.

After our leisurely exploration of the natural wonders this island has to offer, we wander back to the resort hand in hand. It feels comfortable, and somehow right. Maybe I feel this way because I'm far from home, on an island where no one knows me, with a woman who doesn't know me.

Except she does know me a little. I've told her things I haven't told anyone else.

In the lobby, Maddie pulls her hand free of mine. "See you in the morning."

"Morning? No, you can't go. We haven't even had dinner yet."

"I'm pooped, so maybe I'll just order room service."

"We can do that together." Am I desperate to keep her near me? Yes, and I'm not ashamed of that fact. I'll beg if necessary. "Please, Maddie, stay with me."

"For dinner, you mean."

"All night. I promise I won't seduce you, but I'd love to—" I stop mid-sentence as I realize what I intend to say next. I can't believe I'm about to suggest it, but I will suggest it. I want this more than I've wanted anything in a long time. "I'd love it if you stayed with me in my suite for the duration. For the whole two weeks. Just sleeping together, actually sleeping, is all I want for tonight."

She stares at me, not blinking, her lips parted.

Maybe I've stunned her so badly she can't comprehend what I've said. I can't quite comprehend it either. Just sleep with her? All night? She won't be sore for more than a few days, I imagine, but I absolutely would love to spend every night with her body cradled against mine while we sleep.

"It's too much, isn't it?" I ask, though I'm hoping she'll disagree with me.

Maddie bites her upper lip, still eying me with a strange expression.

Now I've ruined it. She's horrified, and she's about to tell me to sod off. Well, being American, she'll probably tell me to go to hell.

A smile stretches her lips little by little. "I would love to do that. Should I give up my room?"

"That's up to you. Dane and Rika are paying for it, after all. If you want to keep it strictly so they won't be offended, that's your decision."

"Rika doesn't need to know. She's my sister, not my keeper."

"You're doing it, then? Moving in with me?"

Her smile gets even bigger, so bright that her happiness warms me too. "Yes, I'm moving in with a guy I just met. I've lost my mind, but this feels too damn good to question it. I'll give up my room in case someone else needs it. The resort did overbook once. They might do it again."

We've both lost our minds, apparently, but I agree with Maddie. This feels too good to worry about it. I don't want to worry about anything for these two weeks. Why should I worry? I have an incredible woman who wants to share my suite and my bed, even if we don't have sex.

"I'll help you get your things," I say, "and bring them to my—*our* suite. Do you think I need to inform the resort that you'll be staying with me?"

"Probably. They'll charge more for a second occupant, I'm sure."

"Let's take care of that first."

"You go do that while I shove my stuff into suitcases." She kisses me and pats my chest. "I think you can live without me for ten minutes."

"What if I can't? I might expire right here in the lobby, starved to death by the lack of your presence."

"I think you'll pull through."

She kisses me again and jogs off to her room.

I watch her shapely arse until she turns down a hallway, out of sight.

Once I've informed the desk clerk about the new arrangement, and I've signed a slip of paper to acknowledge I'm willing to pay the extra fees, I sit down on one of the sofas in the large lobby to wait for Maddie. Any amount of money is worth it to have her with me. Of course, the only other time she's been in my suite, we were shagging on every piece of furniture for hours and hours. When she walks into that suite again, I might experience an overpowering urge to reenact last night.

But I won't do it. I'm not a bastard.

No, I will not ravish her tonight. Not even if she calls me Rick in that sultry purr.

I'm contemplating the strength of my willpower when my mobile rings. The second I answer, I wish I hadn't.

"Good day, Mr. Hunter," says a feminine voice I've heard too often lately, so often that I recognize her Austrian accent after hearing her speak four words. "This is Ilsa Weingartner, personal assistant to Sir Dexter Armstrong-Hill."

Oh bloody hell. Why can't I at least get *this* albatross off my neck?

"Good day to you too, Ms. Weingartner," I say, attempting to sound pleasant when all I want to do is disconnect this call, chuck my mobile in the nearest rubbish bin, and find Maddie so I can kiss her senseless. "What can I do for you today?"

"Sir Dexter requests that you dine with him this evening at his home. Eight o'clock. I will text you the dress code."

"Dress code? Sorry, I already have plans. We'll need to reschedule for another time."

"You know how Sir Dexter feels about rejection." Ilsa doesn't sound like she's chastising me. She's simply stating a fact, and yes,

I know exactly how Dexter responds to rejection. He suggests I get drunk, then he belts out bawdy sea shanties until my ears are ringing—and that's how he reacts over the phone. I don't care to find out how he handles rejection in person.

"May I ask what your plans are for this evening, Mr. Hunter?"

"Personal, not business."

"Bring your companion along. Sir Dexter won't mind, as long as only one extra person accompanies you."

How will Maddie feel about that? She might be excited about it, or she might get angry at me for agreeing to a business meeting. This is meant to be a work-free holiday, after all. "I need to discuss this with my, ah, friend. I'll ring you in half an hour with my answer."

Ilsa's voice drops to a whisper. "Please don't make me tell him that. Last time someone delayed accepting his invitation, he drank an entire bottle of cognac and danced nude on the veranda for an hour while reciting filthy limericks."

I do empathize with Ilsa. Her employer is a difficult man at best, though he's also very charming. And yes, Dexter has a filthy mind. No one who hasn't spoken to him would know that, certainly not from reading his books.

Maddie walks into the lobby. Noticing me, she smiles and waves.

"All right," I tell Ilsa while I wave at Maddie. "Let Dexter know we'll be there at eight."

"Thank you, Mr. Hunter. I appreciate your cooperation. The helicopter will pick you up at seven forty-five."

"Goodbye, Ilsa."

I hang up and walk toward Maddie while she walks toward me. We meet halfway, and I instinctively claim her hand. "Where are your bags?"

"A bellboy will bring them. I called the front desk to tell them I don't need the room anymore, but they'd already heard the news." She taps a finger on my chest. "From a British man with a sexy voice."

"I doubt the desk clerk described me that way. He can't be gay considering how much he enjoys staring at women's arses."

"Maybe I added the sexy-voice part." She leans sideways just enough to see my arse. "Well, if that desk clerk didn't ogle your tush, then he's one hundred percent straight. Anyone who likes men wouldn't be able to resist staring at your ass."

"Not sure if I should thank you for that compliment. I can't tell if it *is* a compliment."

"Of course it is." She pats my arse. "You, Richard, have got one fine behind. And I've seen all of it."

"I'm well-acquainted with your behind too, and it's perfection."

"You are so skilled at sucking up. It's impressive."

"Wait until you hear me talking to an author or a literary agent." I groan, because mentioning work reminds me of what I need to tell her. My shoulders sag. "I'm afraid our plans for the evening have been altered. I need to have dinner with a very difficult man so I can try to convince him to sign a contract with my company. His personal assistant just called to inform me that her employer commands me to dine with him at eight o'clock this evening."

Maddie's shoulders sag too. "Can't you say no? You're on vacation."

"This wasn't meant to be a holiday, not in the beginning. I came here to meet this particular author, but he's been…resistant to the idea." I lift her hand to kiss it. "You can come with me."

"To a business dinner? That doesn't sound like a lot of fun."

"Maybe you'll change your mind once I tell you who I'm meeting." I fold both my hands around hers. "Sir Dexter Armstrong-Hill."

Her eyes widen. "The recluse nobody's seen in decades? He's like the Howard Hughes of the publishing world, isn't he? Kind of nutty, super wealthy, and impossible to get hold of."

"That's all true, though I don't think Dexter is quite as bad as Howard Hughes was."

"Dexter Armstrong-Hill hasn't written a book in how long? Must be twenty years at least."

I let go of her hand, stuffing both of mine in my trouser pockets. "It's been almost thirty years. Every publishing company on earth has tried to sweet-talk him into making a comeback. But *he* contacted *me* via his personal assistant. Signing him would be the biggest coup in the history of the publishing industry."

"Really? Well, we have to go."

"Even though I'm breaking my vow to avoid work for two weeks?"

"Plans can change. It's not the end of the world." She throws her arms around me and presses her lips to mine, holding them there for several seconds. "I'd love to go with you. It'll be like an adventure. I assume he lives on this island."

"No, he lives on a private island twenty-five kilometers west of this one. He'll send a helicopter to pick us up."

"Wow, that's even more of an adventure. I can't wait." She twists her mouth one way, then the other. "Do I need to dress up for this? I didn't bring any fancy clothes."

My mobile chimes, and I pull away from Maddie to get it out of my pocket and check the text Ilsa sent me. I wince.

"Dexter's dress code is…unusual," I say. "His personal assistant, Ilsa, texted me the details. We'll need to visit a particular shop to get ready for our adventure. Dexter won't let us inside his home if we aren't wearing the appropriate clothes from the appropriate shop."

"An unusual dress code. This just keeps getting better." She bounces on her toes, clapping her hands—but not loud enough for anyone else to hear. "A mystery dinner with a mysterious man. Let's go."

She is absolutely adorable. So of course, I want to shag her.

But I won't do it tonight. Besides, I suspect Dexter will wear us both out.

Chapter Eleven

Maddie

I skim my hands over my new dress, feeling oddly invigo-rated by the prospect of the mysterious dinner party Richard and I are about to attend. My clothes are, like Richard said, unusual. Still, I kind of like it. How often does a girl get the chance to wear a Victorian-style evening gown? I have a reticule too, which turns out to be a little drawstring purse.

First, we'd gone to a costume shop—yeah, a Caribbean island that caters to beach-loving tourists has a costume shop—so we could dress appropriately. Sir Dexter keeps this shop on retainer or something, so they'll always be ready to provide the costumes he demands his guests wear. He pays for it, so hey, I'll roll with the old-timey flow. We also visit a salon so I can get a period-appropriate makeover. Richard has to put on fake sideburns to make him look more like a Victorian gentleman, or maybe he's a rake. I don't know the difference.

One more time, I glance down to admire my dress. It's white satin with intricate black lace and a neckline that highlights my breasts without exposing too much. I have a pearl necklace too, and pearl earrings to match. I feel like I've just stepped out of a movie. Or maybe I'm stepping into one. I do have a mysterious engagement at the home of a mysterious man.

In his Victorian suit, Richard looks hot enough to set the whole island on fire.

We're standing in the airport waiting for our helicopter to arrive. It feels kind of strange to be dressed like the olden days while gazing out at a Caribbean inlet where speedboats zoom by in the fading twilight and we're waiting for a chopper to pick us up. Any minute I expect to see either a pirate ship dock out there or a TV crew jump out of a closet to announce we're being filmed for a practical-joke show.

I think I'd prefer the pirates.

Neither of those things happens. The helicopter lands, and we climb aboard. I have some trouble with that since I'm wearing voluminous skirts that go down to my feet. Richard has to help me, but finally, we are on our way. The helicopter takes off.

Through the windows, I can see the lights on the boats below us and the stars in the sky above us. I hold my date's hand the whole way because I like doing that, but also because I've never flown in a helicopter before. It's a little scary to see all those lights whizzing by so far beneath us. Though I can't see the water, I know we're flying over open sea when the number of lights from sea vessels dwindles. The glow of the resort retreats from view too.

We don't try to talk to each other during the flight, though we have headsets with mics. I'm engrossed by the night sky. Every time I look at Richard, he's looking at me, smiling, like he's as engrossed by me as I am by the stars and the moon.

Once we're on the ground, we find a horse-drawn carriage waiting for us near the dock. Oil lanterns on poles illuminate the area, and I'm not kidding about our transportation. Two white horses pull a gold-trimmed white carriage that has an interior upholstered in velvet and oil lanterns attached to each of its four corners. The whole scene is like something out of a fairy tale.

Like a perfect Victorian gentleman, Richard offers me his hand to help me into the carriage. I don't think he's playing a part. He is as sweet and courteous as he seems. I can't remember the last time any guy offered me his hand or opened a door for me. Yep, Richard does that too. He held the costume shop door for me, and the salon door too. If he had a cape, I'm sure he would've laid that down on the ground so I wouldn't have to walk on the dirt.

During the carriage ride to Sir Dexter's house, we hold hands again. I scoot closer to him so I can rest my cheek on his shoulder. How can spending time with a man I barely know feel so comfortable? Doesn't matter. This is my first vacation in…ever, I think. I'm going to enjoy it and make the most of every moment.

Soon the trees thin out, revealing a large house with oil lanterns hung across the width of its wraparound porch. More flickering light emanates from inside the house.

"Does this guy have electricity?" I ask Richard.

"I have no idea. I've never been here before."

"Are you sure this guy is worth all the trouble?"

He sighs. "These days, I'm not sure of anything."

The closer we traveled to this house, the edgier he'd gotten. I felt his body stiffening up—and not in the way I like. Now that we're here, and our carriage is rolling to a stop, his shoulders bunch up, and I swear he's clenching his teeth too.

"Are you okay?" I ask while he helps me out of the carriage.

"Fine, yes."

"So you grit your teeth for fun?"

He stares at me for a second, then blows out a big breath. "Sorry. I don't want to ruin the evening for you. I've been courting Dexter for months, but this is the first time I'll meet with him in person. We've spoken on the phone several times. But mostly, I talk to his assistant, Ilsa."

"You're nervous. That's understandable. You've got a lot riding on convincing Dexter to work with you."

"The fate of my company, and all the people we employ, rides on this. Signing him could erase the mistakes I've made."

I slip my hand into his, threading our fingers. "Wish I could help you."

"We met yesterday, so you're under no obligation to do anything for me. But I appreciate your support."

"Maybe I can't convince Dexter to sign a contract with your company, but there is something I can do later." I lean closer and whisper, "I give great massages."

"Since we're not going to have sex, I'd better decline your offer. A massage from you will make me want to do wicked things to your body."

Richard leads me up the porch steps and to the front door. It's huge, taller than both of us combined, I think. He grasps the big gold knocker and raps on the wood.

Maybe two seconds go by before the door swings open.

A pretty woman wearing a scarlet dress—Victorian, of course—offers us a tight smile. "Good evening, Mr. Hunter. And who is your guest this evening?"

She speaks with an accent, German or something. I've never been good at figuring out where someone's from based on their accent. She has golden blonde hair that's pulled up into an intricate style, and her blue eyes focus on Richard and only Richard.

He lays a hand on my back. "This is Dr. Madeleine Solberg."

The woman finally looks at me, one brow arching. "Doctor? Sir Dexter will be impressed you've brought such a high-caliber guest, Mr. Hunter. I am Ilsa Weingartner, personal assistant to Sir Dexter Armstrong-Hill."

She offers me her hand.

I shake it, feeling a little intimidated. This woman is lovely, tall, and elegant, and she carries herself with poise and grace. She looks like she belongs in a Victorian dress, while I suddenly feel like an impostor. "Nice to meet you, Ms. Weingartner."

She nods crisply, then steps aside and waves for us to enter.

We follow Ilsa down a hallway and into a dining room.

A long wooden table fills most of the space, with matching chairs lined up along either side and one at each end. Candelabras sit on the tabletop, arranged in a long row with a few feet between them. Overhead, a crystal chandelier features…light bulbs. They look like LEDs. Okay, our host isn't a Luddite after all.

The table has been set for three.

Ilsa invites us to sit down, making sure we take the chairs on either side of the one at the head of the table. Then she excuses herself and leaves.

"This place is like a museum," I tell Richard, who's skimming his fingers over the myriad silverware. I've never seen so many utensils, and I have no idea what to do with most of them.

Ilsa reappears in the doorway, holding a small silver bell. She rings it.

A man shuffles past her into the room.

"Sir Dexter Armstrong-Hill," Ilsa says like she's announcing the arrival of a guest at a Victorian ball. "Dinner will be served in ten minutes."

The man shuffles down the length of the table to take the seat at the head, where Richard and I are sitting at either side. Sir Dexter Armstrong-Hill has shoulder-length gray hair that's curly and wild, as well as bushy sideburns. He wears an old-timey suit, but it's a bit rumpled. Our host aims his brown eyes at Richard.

"We meet at last," Dexter says, beaming at us. His accent is British, but a little different from Richard's. "So, you're the man who wants to seduce me."

Richard's lips tighten, but otherwise, he keeps his cool. "It's a pleasure to meet you, Sir Dexter. Let me introduce my companion, Dr. Madeleine Solberg."

Dexter swings his gaze to me. His lips gradually curve into a smile of unmistakable interest. The sexual kind. He glances at my cleavage, and his smile gets even warmer. "Well, it's a true pleasure to meet you, my darling."

"Thank you. I'm honored to be your guest, Sir Dexter."

"Just call me Dexter. That goes for both of you. We don't need to be formal, do we?"

"I guess not. You can call me Maddie if you want."

"Maddie." He says my name slowly, almost like he's savoring the syllables. "I could go mad for you, Maddie."

"Uh, thanks." What am I supposed to say? I've never before been hit on by a famously reclusive, famously eccentric author. "I read your books when I was in high school. You're a wonderful writer."

"High school?" He rakes his gaze over me again, paying special attention to my bosom. "That must have been last year."

"She's an adult, Dexter," Richard says.

"Is she?" the recluse asks. "Well, she's exquisite no matter how old she is. What sort of doctor are you, Maddie?"

"Epidemiologist. I have a PhD, not an MD."

"Fascinating." He rests his elbows on the table, leaning toward me. "Tell me all about yourself, pet."

My mouth falls open, clearly expecting me to produce words, but I can't. This is the strangest dinner party I've ever attended. The only other dinner parties I've been to were held by the Dixons. Those were informal, family-friendly occasions.

I get the feeling Sir Dexter will make a lot of bawdy jokes.

Richard clears his throat. "Could we discuss the contract first? That is why I'm here, after all."

"Yes, but you brought a delectable female with you. How can I concentrate on business?" He keeps looking at me even when he's speaking to Richard. "Are you sleeping with her?"

I doubt Dexter can see it because he's laser-focused on me, but Richard's eyes narrow and his lips crimp a teeny bit. He could wreck his chances of signing Dexter if he gets annoyed with the man's overt interest in me and his impertinent questions. Maybe I can defuse the situation.

Slanting toward Dexter, I pat his hand. "A lady never discusses her liaisons, does she? But Richard is my companion for the evening, so for my sake, maybe you could dial it back a notch or two."

"But you are enchanting, pet."

"You're quite a character, Dexter, and I think we could be friends. But I don't date or sleep with men who are older than my grandfather."

He stares at me for a few seconds, his expression inscrutable. Just when I decide I must've offended him, he busts out laughing. "You have spectacular taste in women, Richard. Madeleine is delightful, especially when she insults me. Maybe I am older than your grandfather, Maddie, but I am exceptionally good in bed. Just ask any woman on Elusion Island. You're sure to find one who's gotten a leg over with me since I've enjoyed at least half of the female population."

My mouth doesn't gape this time, but I seem to have lost the ability to blink. My eyes start to burn from the lack of moisture.

Dexter grins at me, and the many wrinkles on his face deepen. "I've shocked you, haven't I? God, I love doing that. Women are delightful when they're stunned."

I can't help laughing. He's obviously teasing me, and I decide he's not a horrible lech after all. He's just a lonely man who hasn't had much company, so he made up a ridiculous lie for fun.

"Not stunned," I say. "It takes a lot more than you've got to shock me."

"Really?"

"Yes, Dexter, really."

"Please, call me Dex." He scoots his chair to the side, moving closer to me. "Now, do tell me everything about yourself. Have you been sunbathing in the nude? I love to do that, and if you're sweet to me, I might take you down to my beach so we can swim together in the nude."

"Will I be invited?" Richard asks. He doesn't sound annoyed anymore. Instead, he looks and sounds amused.

"Everyone is welcome," Dexter says. "Maddie, I'm positive you'd look smashing in a thong bikini."

While Dexter keeps flirting shamelessly, and I keep replying with sassy comebacks, Richard watches me. His lips curl up at the corners. He tips his head to the side just a touch, and faint lines fan out from his eyes.

I've got two men under my spell. Who knew I could do that?

Chapter Twelve

Richard

Sir Dexter Armstrong-Hill is nothing like I expected. Based on our phone conversations, I suppose I should've guessed. But somehow, I'd expected to meet a doddering old man who walks with a cane and talks about how much his arse itches. I loved his books when I was at university but meeting the man has proved…confusing. I have no idea what sort of story he might write these days but signing him could save my company from what Danisha Davies has done to it.

Maddie laughs at something Dexter said. Her eyes sparkle, and her face lights up.

She has a surprising talent for handling Dexter. He makes suggestive remarks, and she blithely replies, not giving a toss if she's insulting him. Most surprising of all, he doesn't take offense. Not ever. Even when she suggests that his "equipment" might be "a little rusty" and then asks if he can still "rev that engine these days," he just laughs and calls her "pet" again.

What an amazing woman she is.

Dinner arrives, and Maddie and I both tell Dexter how wonderful the food is. It seems like restaurant quality. We share a bottle of red wine too, while Dexter and Maddie exchange more banter. I should probably interject myself into the conversation to gently steer it toward business, but I love watching Maddie spar with the man who lives like a recluse but acts like a game-show host.

The more I listen to them, the more I like them both. I'd already become fond of Maddie, but I'm starting to appreciate Dexter's sense of humor too. He's made wooing him, in the business sense, a difficult and frustrating process. But here in his home, he's very personable, even charming.

Once dessert is served, Maddie surprises me yet again by bringing up the topic I've avoided throughout dinner. "Dex, you really should listen to Rick's offer. I'm sure he'll make you a great deal. He's very smart and business savvy, and also very ethical and upfront."

Dexter raises his brows at me. "Are you all of that, Rick?"

He emphasizes my name, probably because I've never told him he could call me Rick. I've always introduced myself as Richard.

"Yes, he is," Maddie says. "That and much more. He won't schmooze you into signing a crummy deal, then turn around and stab you in the back. Richard Hunter is a good man."

And she knows this after less than two days with me? I suspect she's the one schmoozing Dexter, but I appreciate her efforts to help me.

Dexter wags his eyebrows. "All right, Rick. You've got one hour to convince me. Let's take our dessert into the sitting room and enjoy a good cognac to go along with it. Then you can tell me all about what your company can do for me."

He pushes his chair back and stands.

I get up too. "I hope you'll also share with me what your new book will be about."

"Oh, you'll love the story," he says. "It's crackerjack."

We troop across the hall into the sitting room, a cozy space with padded leather chairs, a small sofa, and a fireplace. It's summer, in the Caribbean, and he has a fire flickering in the hearth. I study the flames and realize why they look odd.

"Is that an electric fireplace?" I ask. "It doesn't seem to be giving off any heat, though."

"Of course not," Dexter says like I'm a fool. "It's too hot here in the tropics for a fire. It's there to look pretty."

"The flames are very realistic. About your new book—"

"Dessert first, then business." Dexter smiles. "Dessert and cognac, that is."

He drank enough wine at dinner to make most people tipsy, but he doesn't act like he's overindulged. Maddie consumed less wine than he did, but I'm the teetotaler in the group. I had one glass, no more. Getting pissed when I'm here to negotiate a publishing deal doesn't seem wise, though I have a feeling Dexter wouldn't care. I could strip naked and jump on the coffee table to dance a jig, and our host would probably cheer me on.

Maddie is laughing at something Dexter said. They both look at me with curious expressions.

"Sorry," I tell them. "My mind wandered. What did you say, Dexter?"

"Call me Dex. We're friends now, after all. Any man who brings a luscious woman like Maddie to my home has earned my friendship."

But that friendship doesn't extend to talking about his new book, which is the entire reason I came to the Caribbean. He insisted on it. "In-person negotiations only," he'd said.

I wonder if he'd be this gregarious if I had come alone.

None of the gossip about him mentioned that he's a brazen flirt.

"Sit down," Dexter says, dropping onto a Victorian-style, high-backed chair. He gestures toward the little sofa that's overflowing with throw pillows. "Give your bums a rest."

We've been sitting down all through dinner, so I don't feel like my bum needs rest. I'd rather stand for a bit, but indulging our host seems like the best way to soften him up for negotiations.

So I push a few pillows out of the way and settle onto the sofa.

Maddie sits down beside me and sinks into a pile of pillows. She slips her hand into mine while she offers me a sweetly encouraging smile.

I know she came with me to this so-called meeting because she wanted to meet the mysterious Dexter Armstrong-Hill. But why is she helping me by buttering him up? She hardly knows me. Yet here she is, laughing and drinking with Dexter, telling him I'm a good man.

Our dessert plates and cognac snifters are on the coffee table that separates us from Dexter's chair. He picks up his glass and plate, then Maddie and I do the same. She starts delicately pulling pieces off her little cake, or whatever these confections are, with the tines of her fork. I watch her slide a bite into her mouth and close her lips around the tines. As she withdraws the fork, she shuts her eyes and sighs like it's the most delicious food she's ever put in her mouth.

"Try the cognac," Dexter says. "It goes beautifully with the cakes."

She holds the snifter close to her nose, swirling it gently while she gazes into its depths. "Do I smell figs? Vanilla too, I think, and a whiff of leather. That's weird, but I'm game."

"Take a sip, darling," Dexter instructs, his voice deeper, almost like he's trying to seduce her. "You'll love the way it feels inside you."

Yes, now he's definitely trying to seduce my date. *Cheeky old codger.*

Maddie sips the cognac. Her eyes drift shut again, and her lips curl in a rapturous little smile. "Mm, yes. Sweet and decadent, but with a silky-smooth finish. It's wonderful. The warmth of it glides down my throat and makes me feel...tingly all over." She takes another sip, her smile getting bigger but no less sensual. "Oh my, it's even better the second time. It's like liquid sex."

Christ, her voice and the words she's saying...It sends blood rushing below my waist. Any second, I'll go hard—right here in front of the world's most famous and reclusive author. What a brilliant way to start an important meeting. Well, with Dexter, who knows? He might think it's hilarious, or he might suggest we have a threesome right here in the sitting room.

I'm not sharing Maddie with this old goat. Not even if he promises to sign with my company if I agree to a small orgy. And if he suggests a threesome with him, Maddie, and Ilsa...I just might pummel the lecherous arse. I like Dexter, but not *that* much.

Liquid sex, Maddie said. She sounded like she might climax if she takes another sip of her cognac. Why did I tell her we shouldn't have sex again yet? If there was a reason, I've forgotten it. The way she looks in that old-fashioned dress, and the way she reacted to the cognac, all of it has me ready to throw her over my shoulder, drag her to the nearest unoccupied room, and shag her until she can't move anymore.

Except she's still sore from what I did to her last night. Maybe I'm the lecherous arse in this room.

Maddie slips another, larger bite of cake between her lips, then takes a drink of the cognac while she's still chewing.

Her eyes roll back in her head.

I'm not exaggerating. They do that. The look of unbridled ecstasy on her face has me flashing back to last night when I'd made her look that way while she'd begged me to never stop fucking her.

And now I'm hard. *Bugger.*

Grabbing a throw pillow, I hold it on my lap and set my plate on it. That way it sort of seems like I'm just worried about the plate falling off my thigh, not like I'm so aroused by Madeleine Solberg that I need to hide my raging erection.

Maddie consumes more cake while lacing each bite with cognac from her glass. She exhales a soft moan with every mouthful she swallows.

Dexter chuckles with all the lecherous intent of a randy old goat. "Maddie, you are the most fascinating woman I've ever met. If you get this excited about cognac, you must be the most bloody incredible shag on earth." He glances at me, smirking. "Can you confirm that, Richard?"

"Ah, well…" I scratch under my collar because this sodding costume seems to be made from poison-ivy thread. "I don't kiss and tell."

"We're mates. That means you can tell me anything."

"I'm still not discussing my sex life with you."

He rolls his eyes, turning his attention to Maddie. "Is my mate Rick any good in bed? I certainly hope so. A woman like you needs intense passion in her life. If he can't handle you, I'm ready and willing to take over."

Maddie chokes on the piece of cake she'd been chewing. Coughing, she swigs her cognac. That makes her cough even more.

I pat her back, and I wonder why people do that when someone is hacking. Does that actually help? I doubt it.

Dexter hurries over to a drinks cabinet in the corner. "I've got some mineral water in here. Let me get that for you, Maddie."

He digs around inside the cabinet until he finds a glass bottle full of clear liquid. Hustling back to us, he hands the water to her. "Small sips, dear."

She heeds his advice, taking dainty sips until her coughing subsides. "Thank you for the offer, Dex, but I'm good."

Our host smirks again, his eyes twinkling with humor. "You mean Richard is good. Glad to hear it. I can't stand to see a woman whose passion goes unexplored, like a secret map that no man dares to read."

A secret map? Maddie's body is not a secret to me. I know every millimeter of it by heart.

Dexter looks at me. "Would you mind if I dance with your lover?"

"She's my date for tonight. The rest is none of your concern." I set my plate on the table. "And it's Maddie's choice whether she dances with you, not mine."

The woman in question leans in to whisper in my ear, "Sure you won't be jealous if I do? He strikes me as the hold-her-close kind of dance partner."

"I'm not jealous," I hiss out of the corner of my mouth. "Dance with whoever you want."

"Might be good for your business deal if I indulge him a little, but I'd much rather twirl around the room in your arms."

She smiles, squeezes my thigh, and tells Dexter, "I'd love to take a spin with you."

He rises and winks at her. "I love to dip women—deeply. Get a much better view of their tits that way."

Dexter grabs a remote control off the table and clicks buttons until a waltz begins to play through the speakers in the corner. He offers Maddie his hand. She accepts it, and they walk to the open area past the coffee table. Together, they assume the standard, genteel ballroom stance that keeps their hands in plain sight. They dance like that for about thirty seconds.

Then he pulls her snug against his body and slides his hand down to her arse.

Oh yes, he's a cheeky codger for sure.

Chapter Thirteen

Maddie

exter twirls me around in the small area in which we dance. Despite the fact he has his palm on my ass and I'm crushed against his body, he dances like a gentleman—elegant and courteous, never dragging me across the floor, but always leading the way. He's a superb dancer, but the whole time we're waltzing, I keep wondering what it would feel like to dance with Rick like this. Does he know how to waltz? I don't, so I'm faking it by following Dex's lead.

He might be a dirty-minded senior citizen, but he's also a sweet man. He genuinely seems to care if Richard and I have good sex. I've decided that's his way of expressing his belief that we make a good couple.

Do we? I think so, but I have no idea what Rick thinks.

As the beautiful music winds down, Dexter dips me. Deeply, just like he swore he would. But he's not ogling my boobs. He's smiling at Richard.

"Your turn, Rick," our host says. "I bet you'll dip her thoroughly tonight, won't you?"

I can't see Richard, since I have my head tipped backward away from that part of the room. I hope he's not annoyed that I called him Rick in front of Dexter, who now loves to use that nickname. Richard accepted our host's offer to call him Dex, so I'm guessing he'll be okay with the Rick thing.

Dex pulls me up out of the dip and steps away from me, holding my hand up. "Get over here and claim her, Rick. She's a stimulating partner."

Rick swallows the last of his cognac, clears his throat, and walks over to us.

Dexter grasps Rick's hand, raising it, and places mine in his palm.

"There," Dexter says. "Enjoy holding her against you. She's a treasure. I'll start the music for you."

Our host returns to his chair, grabbing the remote for the stereo.

Richard cautiously lays a hand on my lower back. Once I place my hand on his shoulder, the music starts up. Another waltz. He whirls me around and around, his gaze capturing mine, his lips curved in a subdued smile. I love the sensation of his hand on my back, and I wish he'd take a cue from Dexter and slide that hand lower to cup my bottom. I didn't mind when Dex did that, but I'd love for Rick to touch me that way.

He doesn't, though. He keeps a small gap between us and keeps his hands right where they're supposed to be.

I can't resist slanting closer to murmur, "Waltzing was a scandalous act back in Victorian days. Being so close to your partner meant you were the worst kind of rake."

"Yes, I read an article from the eighteen-sixties that explained how waltzing could cause sickness because holding a woman too near your body will inevitably lead to intercourse later in the evening. And syphilis was a serious concern." He draws me closer, our bodies pressed together. "I'm beginning to understand why the author of that article made that claim. Dancing with you is almost as sensual as making love."

"I didn't feel that way when I danced with Dex." I glide my hand across his shoulder, spreading my fingers over his throat. "But with you, I'm getting warm all over."

"As much as I want you, Madeleine, I can't do it. You need time to recover."

"We can do things that don't involve penetration. I've got lots of ideas about that."

He chuckles, too softly for Dexter to have heard. "You have quite the appetite, don't you?"

"Am I being too forward? I'm not usually like this, but I can't help it when I'm with you." I tickle his neck with my fingertips. "If you don't want me to seduce you, better stop being so irresistible."

"I'm not complaining. I love your passion."

Glass clinking spurs us both to glance toward Dexter.

He's holding his snifter, tapping it with his fork. "You two look about ready to retire for the evening. And by 'retire' I mean shagging in your room. You are staying the night, aren't you?"

Richard freezes, forcing me to halt too. "I'd assumed the helicopter would take us back to the resort."

"I could call the pilot to retrieve you, but I'd much rather you both stay here. I have plenty of room. Then we can discuss your offer in the morning."

"But I thought we would talk about that tonight."

Richard's body has tensed up like he's anxious about the business deal. Maybe he worries Dexter will put him off again in the morning. He did say he's been courting Dex for a while without any luck.

I approach Dexter, leaning forward to touch his arm. I know I'm also giving him a good look at my cleavage, and yeah, I do that on purpose. What's the use of having tits if I can't use them to help my boyfriend? If Richard is my boyfriend. Maybe we're just lovers.

Ugh. Like that matters right now.

With my cleavage in full view, I say, "Please, Dex, don't make Rick wait until morning. He came all this way to meet you. As a favor to me, talk to him now."

His focus gravitates to my chest. "I never can say no to a beautiful woman in a Victorian gown. All right, let's discuss this publishing rubbish."

I kiss his cheek. "Thank you, Dex. You're a sweetie."

"Does that mean we can get a leg over while Rick is asleep?"

Shaking my head, I grab Richard's hand and lead him back to the sofa. Once we've sat down, Dex pours us each another glass of cognac.

"Business meetings require liquor," he declares.

"Only in the Caribbean," Richard says. He takes a tiny sip. "Why don't you tell me about your new book? You've been rather cagey about the storyline. In fact, you've told me nothing except that it will be 'glorious' and 'crackerjack.' I'm anxious to hear more about it."

Dexter swigs his cognac, swallowing almost all of it. With a satisfied sigh, he relaxes into his chair. "I suppose it is time I share the details."

Rick seems to be clenching his jaw, and his hand on his thigh is tense too, his fingers crooked into his leg. Jeez, he's way more anxious about this than I realized. So I lay my hand over his, rubbing my thumb in slow circles until his fingers relax.

"All right, the story," Dexter says while he swirls the remaining cognac in his glass. "I've taken a different approach with this book. It's quite a departure from my previous works, but there's a good reason for that. I got so bloody sick of writing literary novels about blokes who wander about here, there, and everywhere searching for meaning in life. Do you want to know the real answer to that question? What is the meaning of life?"

A muscle ticks in Richard's jaw, and his fingers start to crook into his thigh again.

I peel his hand away from his leg and thread my fingers with his.

He exhales the breath he must've been holding and flashes me a grateful smile. "Go on, Dex. Share the meaning of life with us."

"It's bollocks. There is no overarching plan, no soul-inspiring insight. You're born, you shag, you die. The end."

Rick screws up his mouth. "I think I saw that on a T-shirt. Now, are you going to tell me about your book or not? I flew here from England just to hear this."

"But Madeleine must've been expecting a tropical holiday, not a business meeting. Why else would she travel here with you?"

"The book, Dex. Now."

Our host simply smiles, the expression as inscrutable as the man himself. I'm getting the idea that Dex likes to keep people wondering, possibly because he enjoys the attention. He must be lonely living here with only a small staff. I assume he has that staff since it's clear someone cleans the house and cooks the meals. Plus, an older woman served our dinner.

Though it's not my business, maybe I can assist Richard in this discussion. Dex likes me, and I like him, so I've got a bit of leverage here.

I hold up my empty snifter. "Would you mind if I have a little more of your delicious cognac, Dex?"

He lights up, leaning forward to pick up the bottle. "Of course, dear Madeleine. I'm glad you like it. This bottle cost two thousand East Caribbean dollars."

While he refills my glass, I sit there frozen. "Two thousand? How much is that in American dollars?"

"I've no idea."

"Eight hundred American dollars," Rick says.

I glance down at my now-full glass. "Holy shit. That's still a lot of money. The most expensive bottle of wine I ever bought cost ninety dollars."

Dexter holds the bottle out to Richard. "Care for a little more? I love burning through money, but drinking it is even better."

"No, thank you. About your manuscript…"

"Relax, Rick, I'll tell you soon enough." He winks. "But let's watch Maddie enjoy liquid sex before we get back to business."

My boyfriend, or whatever he is to me, clenches his jaw and his hands, tightening those into fists on his thighs. Either Dex doesn't notice, or he doesn't care.

I kiss Rick's cheek and whisper into his ear, "I'll handle this."

Yeah, I can handle Dex. But it might require a small sacrifice, one that involves doing something I've never done before.

That's right. To spare Richard from potential murder charges, if Dex keeps stringing him along, I will get drunk. Well, tipsy. I already feel looser than usual thanks to the cognac, but I'm willing to go all the way to get this done.

I throw back my entire glass of cognac in one gulp. It sizzles down my throat and rushes through my system with a heady warmth that incongruously makes me shiver. "Ooh, that's wonderful. I love this stuff even more with every new glassful." I thrust my snifter out toward Dex. "More, please."

"Haven't you had enough?" Rick asks.

"Mm-mm. I need more." Do I sound like a lusty coed at her first frat party? Yeah, I am lusting after that cognac. And Rick. How much fun would it be to pour cognac all over his body and lick it all up? Lots, I'm sure. So I hold out my snifter. "Hit me again,

Dex. Make it a double. Or whatever comes after double. Tribble? Something like that."

He pours me another glass of yummy liquid heaven. His smile carves out dimples in his cheeks. He looks like Santa Claus, except for that naughty glint in his eyes and the Victorian outfit he's wearing. If he'd lived way back when, Dexter would've been the wickedest rake in London.

I knock back the entire glass in one swallow, giggling and shivering. "Oh wow, I love it more every time I take it into my mouth. I'm getting kind of tingly all over."

And that feeling makes me look at Rick. Or Richard. Which does he prefer? I can't remember right now, so I'll call him Rick. It's a sexy, sexy, hot and sexy name. If Rick had lived in ye olden days, he would've been the man every woman wants to marry and shag and do…uh, other stuff with. My thoughts are getting kind of fuzzy, and my body feels soft and warm, but I kind of like this. A massage in a bottle, that's what this cognac is. A naughty massage.

I want Rick to give me one of those. Right now. On the coffee table.

Wow, who knew getting bombed could make me so horny? Not that I am bombed. I don't think I am, but…whatever.

Dex offers me the bottle. "Want the rest, lovey?"

"Yes," I say, the last letter drawn out into a hissing sound.

Rick snatches the bottle away before I can grab it. Though I had reached for the bottle, my fingers kept scooting right past it for some weird reason.

Is this a buzz? People talk about that, but I've never gotten tipsy before, so I have no idea what a buzz feels like. Whatever you call it, me want more.

"She's had enough," Rick declares.

I giggle and hiccup. "Okay-okay, I'm done."

"Glad to hear it." Rick sets the bottle on the table.

I wag a finger at Dexter. "Oh now, Dexy, you naughty boy. Tell Rick what he wants to know. He won't give up until you do. And he won't take me to our room and screw me for hours and hours until you tell him about your bookie thingy. He's fabulous in the sack, so I'm dying for him to shag me again. Isn't that just the cutest word for sex? Shag. Shagging. Shagged. Shaggeth? No, that doesn't sound right."

Did I say all that out loud?

Rick gapes at me.

Okay, guess I did say that out loud.

Dexter busts out laughing.

"This is not amusing," Rick says. "You've enabled her to get drunk. I should've stopped this before you gave her more cognac."

"All right, don't have kittens about it," Dexter says. He pulls out the drawer in the little table beside his chair and brings out a big stack of letter-size sheets of paper. Setting that on his lap, he lays a hand atop the stack. "Here's the manuscript. It's a work of carnivalesque erotica titled *Under the Satyr's Moon*, which explores the sexual appetites of a group of people who meet at a fete in a small English village and proceed to turn it into a devilish festival of lust."

Rick stares at Dex. He doesn't blink—or breathe, it seems like. He just sits there with his hands clamped over his knees, bent forward slightly. "Carnivalesque what?"

"Erotica." Dex offers the manuscript to Rick. "Take your time reading it."

"Is this a joke?" he asks as he gingerly takes the stack of papers, setting it on his lap.

"No joke. It's what I've written."

I giggle again, but it mutates into all-out guffaws with a few more hiccups in there too. Now I'm laughing so hard my stomach muscles start to cramp up, and I collapse against the sofa with tears streaming down my cheeks.

"Best take her to bed," Dex announces. "She needs a good lie-in."

Though my tears blur my vision, I can tell Rick is still looking shell-shocked.

I intend to lean toward Rick, but instead, I fall over and wind up with my face in his lap. Yeah, I've face-planted on that manuscript. It smells nice. "Please, take me to bed, Rrrrrick."

Why that syllable comes out so long, I have no idea.

"Yes, I think it is Maddie's bedtime," Rick says.

"I asked Ilsa to make sure a room would be ready for you two," Dexter replies. "Just in case."

My eyes drift closed. He pulls the manuscript out from under my face, and I hear a rustling sound, but I have no idea what it is. He's jostling me too, but only a teeny bit.

He picks me up and stands. "Could you point me in the right direction?"

"Up the stairs, third door on the left."

"Thank you. Good night, Dexter."

As he carries me away, I fling out an arm to wave at our host, with my eyes still closed. I'm guessing about which direction to wave. "Nightie-night, Dexy."

He chuckles. "Good night, Maddie."

I throw my arm around Rick's neck. The other arm seems to be stuck, trapped between his body and mine. "Make love to me, Rrrrrick."

"Yes, Rick, you do that," Dexter says.

A door slams shut. I think that might mean Rick slammed the sitting-room door. Oh, whatever. I feel like liquid sex now, all hot and soft and…What was I thinking about?

I hear his footsteps on the stairs, but he manages to hold me so I don't bounce at all or fall out of his arms. Wow, he's got skills. Is that the right word? Not sure. Skills. The word sounds weird, like it's not actually a word after all.

When he lays me down on the bed, I moan and cuddle up with the pillow.

And I fall asleep.

Chapter Fourteen

Richard

Madeleine Solberg got plastered tonight. I wonder if she's never done that before since she seemed rather…surprised by the feeling. She's always wonderful to be with, but seeing her like this, I can't help being charmed by her drunken antics. She's lying on the bed, on top of the covers, still drowned in layers of Victorian clothing. I can't leave her like that, can I? This house does seem to have air conditioning, but still, she might get overheated with all that fabric suffocating her.

Yes, that's the reason I decide to undress her. For her health.

I behave like a perfect gentleman and do not stare at her naked body.

Well, not for more than ten seconds.

Once I've got her settled, I undress and join her in the large four-poster bed. The sheets feel so silky that I wonder if they are silk. Dexter clearly has money, lots of it, based on this enormous house and the fact he owns the entire island. The man did win the Nobel Prize for Literature, though that happened decades ago. His novels continue to sell, so I have no doubts he earned most, if not all, of his obvious wealth. Did he inherit more? Invest brilliantly? I have no idea, but it doesn't matter.

For an hour, I slog through Dexter's new novel. When my eyes get so dry that they start to burn, I give up and crawl under the covers with Maddie. I fall asleep while thinking about her, what we're doing together, how I might feel when it all ends. Does it need to end? I hardly know her, but I already want to spend more than two weeks with the clever, enchanting woman in the blue bikini.

When I wake up in the morning, Maddie is still sleeping, lying on her side facing me. Her mouth has fallen open. Saliva dribbles from the corner of it while she snores like a snorting pig. Even that enchants me. She's so…lovable, in every way.

Never in my life have I become enamored of a woman I've known for a few days, but I love the way it feels to let go of my inhibitions, forget about work, and do whatever the bloody hell I want. It's reckless and selfish, but I don't care.

Today, I plan to have fun with Maddie. Nothing else. Just fun.

Lying on my side, I watch her sleep. She stops snoring, though her mouth still gapes open. I'd love to kiss her, but I won't disturb her after the night she had. Did she get drunk as a ploy to convince Dexter to tell me about his book? I wondered about that last night. She'd been a touch tipsy before then, but when Dex got cagey about the book, Maddie volunteered to pour cognac down her throat. I suspect she doesn't drink much as a rule, but last night, she made an exception.

Why? Part of me wants to believe she did it for my sake.

Maddie sighs and closes her mouth. Her body moves under the covers like she's trying to stretch but hasn't woken up enough to do that. When she yawns and shrugs her shoulders, the sheet slips off them. But when she rolls onto her back and stretches her entire body, arching her spine, the sheet slides down to her waist.

I get a spectacular view of her tits.

"Good morning," I say. "Sleep well? You must've done since you passed out the second I set you down on the bed and haven't opened your eyes since."

"Mm, I did sleep good." She yawns again, bigger than the first time, and aims her beautiful eyes at me. "Good morning, Rick."

I move to kiss her.

She throws a hand up between our mouths. "I haven't brushed my teeth yet."

"Don't care."

"I do. Morning breath is not attractive, especially when it's coupled with a bender the previous night." She winces. "I acted like a total goofball, didn't I? Ugh. But at least Dexter gave you his book. Have you read it yet?"

"Started on it, yes. How much do you remember about last night?"

"All of it. I wasn't totally wasted." She rubs her eyes with the heels of her hands, then looks at me. "Sorry I acted like such an idiot. I was trying to help you."

"It's all right. You were not an idiot. Quite the contrary. You were the most charming drunk I've ever seen." I kiss her cheek. "And the sexiest."

She licks her lips, grimaces, and wipes her mouth with the sheet. "God, can this get any more embarrassing? I drooled, didn't it?"

"Only while you were asleep."

"Well, I guess that's something to be thankful for." She glances around like she's looking for something until her gaze lands on the old-fashioned wind-up clock on the bedside table. Her eyes go wide. "Is that really the time?"

"Yes, it's half ten."

"But I never, ever sleep until ten thirty." She stares at the clock for a few seconds, then her entire body relaxes, melting her shocked expression. "This is amazing. I slept late, and I don't feel even a twinge of guilt."

"No reason to feel guilty. You're on holiday, after all." I tug the sheet up to cover her breasts. "Why did you pour cognac down your throat to help me with Dexter?"

"Because I figured he'd like watching me get tipsy, and then he'd be in a better mood and decide to talk business after all."

"I understand that bit. But why do that for *me?* We hardly know each other."

"Because I like you."

"I like you too. Very much."

Her lips curl into a sweet smile.

Someone knocks on the door.

"Breakfast," Ilsa calls out to us. "Should I bring it in or leave it at the door?"

"Leave it, please," I say. "Thank you, Ilsa."

"You're welcome."

I crawl out of bed and retrieve the tray of food Ilsa left for us. There's also a folded piece of paper on the tray. Once I've gotten back into bed with Maddie, with the tray over my lap, I open the folded paper.

"What's that?" Maddie asks, pushing up to sit beside me. "The bill for breakfast?"

She's smirking, so I know she's joking. Sir Dexter Armstrong-Hill would never make anyone pay for a meal in his house. I deduced that fact after spending a few hours with the man. He might be strange and often frustrating, sometimes even infuriating, but he treats his guests well.

"No, it's not the bill," I say. "It's a note from Dexter inviting us to join him on the veranda whenever we're ready."

Maddie leans into me, peering down at the paper in my hand. "He has beautiful handwriting. Mine is terrible."

"Isn't that a requirement for being a doctor?"

"Ha-ha. I'm not a medical doctor, anyway. I have a PhD."

"Yes, I remember. But you save lives all the same, don't you?"

"Not the way you and Rika make it sound. My job is primarily research." She plucks the silver lid off the plate that sits on the tray. "Ooh, yum. That looks delicious."

"The end of the note tells us what the food is." I squint at the smaller words at the bottom of the page. "Can't tell what it says without my reading glasses."

"Allow me." She takes the note. "Blue cheese quiche. Waffle sandwiches with avocado and arugula. Mixed berries with mint leaves. Mimosas made with apple cider instead of champagne." She puckers her lips like she's trying not to smile. "And finally, chocolate coffee for the lovely lady who overindulged last night."

"I don't see how we can eat all of this."

"Maybe Dex will give us a doggy bag."

"He just might." I consider the meal laid out on the tray. "There's only one mimosa and one cup of coffee."

"We can share." She lifts the coffee cup to my lips. The whipped cream on top grazes my mouth. "Go on, Richard, have the first sip."

"You can call me Rick all the time if you want. I like the way you say it." I take a sip of the coffee since Maddie is tipping the cup toward my mouth. If I don't drink it, the coffee will wind up dribbling down my chin and onto my chest. "I've never had chocolate coffee before. It's surprisingly good."

She samples the drink. "Mm, yum. Let's try the mimosa next."

"Will you call me Rick? More than once, I've said you can."

Laughing, she grabs a napkin off the tray and wipes my mouth with it, then hers. "Yes, I'll call you Rick. Happy now?"

"I am. Thank you." I have no idea why it's important to me that she calls me Rick, but I feel relieved when she agrees to do that. It's ridiculous. But I decide I've needed more ridiculousness in my life. And besides, who gives a toss? She's the only one who'll know I practically begged her to use my nickname.

Maddie spears the quiche with a fork, tears off a piece, and holds it near my mouth.

I can't resist her, whether she's tempting me with her body or with food, so I eat the mouthful of quiche. "That's good too. You should try it."

She eats a bite, humming her approval. "How did you like Dex's book?"

"Ah…it's interesting."

"That doesn't sound like a rave review."

"It's all about sex. A clown shags a bearded lady while they're riding the ghost train, then he runs off and shags the bloke who does the magic show. After that, he runs into a complete stranger who turns out to be a hermaphrodite, and they do it several times in ways that seem physically impossible. That's as far as I've gotten." I groan and rub my forehead. "How can I publish this? It's not Dexter Armstrong-Hill material. It's fluff that belongs in an adult magazine."

"Doesn't sex sell? That's what I've always heard."

"That's not the point. I can't publish this book. Everyone will expect Dexter to produce another poignant work of literary fiction, not a collection of erotica that has no discernible plot. It's one sex scene after another. The characters barely speak to each other, and all the protagonist thinks about is who he can get a leg over with next."

"Is it badly written?"

Shrugging, I grab a waffle sandwich and shove a huge bite of it into my mouth. And I speak while I'm still chewing. "No idea. Can't see past the bizarre sex."

"How many chapters did you read?"

I hold up four fingers while I devour the rest of my waffle sandwich. The food is excellent, but I have no ruddy clue what to do about Dexter's book.

"Let me read it," Maddie says. "I'm sure Dex won't mind, and maybe I can help you figure out what to do."

"I'm meant to read it. I am the publisher, after all."

"But you're getting so stressed out about this." She settles her head on my shoulder. "Let me help you. Please. I want to do it."

"You're volunteering to read about carnival people having sex in bizarre places?"

"Sure. Why not?"

I shake my head. "Can't believe Dexter wrote that rubbish."

"Let me read the rest of it, then we'll decide if he's trying to feed you a load of garbage. Okay?"

"All right. I should pay you as my consulting editor."

"I don't want you to pay me. This isn't business. I'm doing it for *you*, because I like you and want to help."

"That's very generous, Maddie." I hook an arm around her waist and pull her close. "Let's finish our breakfast, then play silly buggers all day. We can worry about Dex's book later."

"Play what?" she asks with a laugh.

"Silly buggers. It means let's behave like silly, annoying fools who don't care about anything except having a jolly good time."

"I'm all in for that."

While she feeds me a blackberry with a mint leaf on top, I consider what we should do today. Yesterday, we made a list of the activities we wanted to try, which were all things neither of us has ever done before. It's an exhaustive list. Deciding on a starting point is a hard choice.

Once we've finished our breakfast, Maddie wants to have a shower. I want to join her, but she issues a command I can't refuse—because she's so adorably convincing. She says I need to ring my father and "rip that scab off." By that, she means I need to inform him of what's going on with the Danisha Davies book.

I expect him to shout at me. Why, I have no idea. Edward Hunter never shouts or gets boiling mad. But when I ring him, I still expect anger in response. After I've explained the situation, my father stays silent for what feels like an eternity, though it's only a few seconds.

"That's what you have solicitors for, Rick," he finally says. "You did nothing wrong. Now you know about it, and I'm sure you'll take care of things the best way you can."

"What if the company folds because of my mistake?"

"You haven't made a mistake. That woman conned you. Now go enjoy your holiday and worry about this when you're home."

"But I've let you down."

"No, you've never done that, and you never will. I'm very proud of the job you've done since taking over as publisher."

"Thank you for the vote of confidence, but I've only done my job. No more, no less."

"Hogwash."

The fact my father is proud of me lifts a weight off my shoulders. Maybe I haven't bollocksed everything up after all.

We talk for a few more minutes until Maddie walks out of the bathroom, then I say goodbye to my father. Maddie and I help each other get back into our costumes from last night since that's all we have to wear. My clothing proves much easier to reassemble than hers. It has so many strings and clasps or whatever they are that I'm amazed she managed to get into it in the first place. An employee at the costume shop helped her the first time. I clearly lack the expertise to get it done, though, since the task takes me fifteen minutes. At the shop, it took five minutes at most.

"That was a workout," Maddie says when she's finally dressed. She twirls once, making her skirts flutter. "How do I look?"

"You're always lovely, even when you're drooling and snoring."

"Did I really do that? I know I drooled, but the snoring…"

"Yes, you did that. But it was endearing."

"Maybe you're full of shit, but I've decided that's part of your appeal." She slips her arms around my waist. "Let's go snorkeling first."

"Anything you want. We'll need to go back to the resort and change out of these clothes, though."

My mobile chimes. Reluctantly, I step away from her so I can dig it out to check the new text.

Have you signed him? my executive assistant asks. *Board waiting to hear.*

She's referring to Dexter. I type my response: *Working on it. On holiday now.*

Then I stuff the mobile in my pocket.

"By the way," I tell Maddie, "I took your advice and rang my father. He's not angry. He says he's proud of me."

"That's wonderful. Aren't you glad you ripped that scab off?"

"Yes, you were right about that."

She slips her hand into mine. "Let's go downstairs and tell Dexter to bring that chopper back here for us."

I wrap an arm around Maddie and tug her close. "Thank you for coming here with me. This was intended to be a business trip, but you're making it the best holiday I've ever had."

"You're doing the same for me. Thank you, Rick."

While I lead her out of our room and downstairs, I can't help smiling. This woman makes me feel lighter, like all the duties that used to weigh me down have evaporated and all that matters is living life to the fullest.

About damn time.

Chapter Fifteen

Maddie

We find Dexter on the veranda, relaxing on a porch swing and admiring the view from the sheltered peace of this outdoor haven attached to the house. I hadn't really known what a veranda was until today. It's a fancy word for a wraparound porch as far as I can tell. This one stretches the entire length of the house and seems to continue around the backside. While Rick guides me toward Dex, I gaze out at the beach and the blue waters of the inlet. A balmy breeze whispers over my skin. The smell of the ocean surrounds me, and I inhale a deep breath to appreciate that unique scent.

Will I ever smell that again once I go back to work? I doubt I'll ever feel as relaxed and happy as I do today, here with Rick in this tropical paradise.

When Dexter spots us, he smiles. "Good morning, young lovers. Did you sleep well?"

Rick's brows lift slightly. "Young lovers? That might apply to Maddie, but I'm far from young."

"You're not old," I say. "Forty *is* young."

"That's right," Dexter says. "Forty is the new twenty, haven't you heard? Middle age isn't until you're at least seventy."

I wonder how old Dexter is, but I would never ask him. That would be disrespectful. Instead, I say, "Thank you for letting us stay the night in your beautiful home, and for giving us a wonderful breakfast. You are a gracious and charming host, Dex."

"And you are a beautiful and enchanting guest, Madeleine." Dexter gets to his feet, stretching and groaning like it feels so good. "You two should explore the island today. Relax on the beach. Or better yet, make love on the beach."

Rick's mouth drops open, but he just stares at Dex.

Since he seems incapable of speaking, I tell our host, "We were planning to go back to the resort."

"Nonsense," Dexter says. "You'll have a much better time here. More privacy too."

"That's generous, but we don't want to impose."

"It's not an imposition. I'm enjoying having you two here to breathe new life into this old house." He points at himself. "And this old bloke."

I glance at Rick. "What do you think? There is a nice, secluded beach."

"We don't have swimsuits. Or any normal clothing."

"Tosh," Dex announces. "I have a collection of fresh new clothing on hand for my guests, including swimwear. Ilsa can show you. And besides, you can always swim in the nude."

Richard makes a noise, but it's not a word. It sounds like a gasp that he tried to swallow.

I hook my arm under his. "Just think, we could go snorkeling without anybody bothering us."

Dexter's expression brightens. "Snorkeling? I have the best beach in the Caribbean, with a pristine coral reef and more varieties of fish than you can count. I've owned this island for thirty years, and I've hired the best people to ensure the environment is protected. You won't have a better experience anywhere else."

"Let's stay," I tell Rick.

"All right," he agrees. "A private island does sound more appealing than a crowded resort."

"Definitely." I switch to a whisper that only Rick will hear. "After we have our fun, I'll read Dex's book. Then we can talk about it—and talk to him. Okay?"

He nods.

"A secret conversation?" Dexter says. "How titillating. By the way, I'll be popping over to Elusion Island for a video chat with my grandchildren. We don't have internet here since I don't like using it. You may have noticed there is a cellular signal, but it's not strong enough to do that online rubbish. There is satellite telly, of course, though only in my bedroom and only so I can watch cricket matches. Am I prattling on like an old fool? So sorry."

"Don't apologize," I say. "If babbling is a crime, I'm guilty too."

"You are such a love, Maddie." He grimaces. "I hope my little darlings haven't invited their grandmother to participate in the chat. My ex-wife loves to commandeer the webcam after the children leave and chastise me for all my old sins."

"I'm sure you can handle that, Dex."

Our host smiles and ambles into the house.

"Should we take Dexter's suggestion and swim naked?" I ask. "I've never gone skinny dipping. Have you?"

"No, I never had the chance."

"Let's do it, then. But first, we probably should grab different clothes and some towels."

"Definitely."

We find Ilsa in the downstairs hallway. She happens to be walking in our direction right when we reenter the house.

"Good morning, Ilsa," Rick says. "Dex mentioned you could point us toward his special closet for guests. We need a change of clothes."

"Oh yes, of course," she says, waving toward the other end of the hallway. "Follow me."

She leads us to the door at the end of the hall and swings it open.

Holy moly, it's the hugest closet I've ever seen. Racks and racks of clothing fill the space, everything from swimsuits to formal wear.

"Dexter is so pleased you're staying on," Ilsa says. "Please take anything you like from the guest wardrobe. Whatever you select is yours to keep."

"That's incredibly generous. Is this all designer stuff?"

"Mostly. Dexter doesn't care about labels, though. He wants to provide attractive, comfortable clothing for his guests, whether they're here for the night or the week."

Yesterday, she called our host Sir Dexter. Today, she's ditched the honorific. My scientist brain wants to ask her about that, but it would be rude. After all, I'm the woman who stole my one-night lover's wallet so I could find out his name. Yeah, I still feel bad about that.

Richard Hunter is not my one-night lover anymore. He's…something else.

"Dexter must have a lot of guests," I say.

"Not crowds of them," Ilsa tells me. "But he does love it when someone visits. He can be particular about who he allows on the island, so it's an honor to be invited."

"Yes, it is," Rick agrees. "And we are very grateful for the hospitality both you and Dex have shown us."

"Absolutely," I chime in.

Ilsa smiles and gestures toward the wardrobe room. "I will leave you to explore. When you're ready to go to the beach, just follow the trail from the west veranda."

"Thank you, Ilsa," Rick says.

While she heads back down the hall, Richard and I wander into the wardrobe room. I have no idea where to start since I'm surrounded by clothing. Then I notice the little signs on top of the racks. Someone has labeled them with the type of clothing each contains, everything from "swimwear for ladies" to "suits for gents." I amble over to the women's swimwear and flip through the options, which are all carefully clipped onto hangers.

Rick is on the other side of the room examining the men's options for beach attire. Several racks stand between us, so I can't see much other than his head.

"Are we dressing for the beach?" I call out to him. "Or are we swimming naked? I only ask because the answer will change what kind of clothes I choose."

He lifts his head to look at me, and his lips slide into a naughty smile. "Wear a bikini, but only so I can watch you strip it off once we're at the beach."

"See any skimpy, super-tight options over there? If so, wear one. Then I can watch you peel it off your body."

I choose a swimsuit—a bikini, per his request—that has a beautiful, bright flower-print pattern. Instead of a string bikini, I've chosen one with a halter top and a high-cut bottom. After I pull on the swimsuit, I tie a sarong around my hips, slung low, and slip on a pair of cute flip-flops that have fake flowers sewn onto them.

"Ready?" I ask, almost shouting to make sure he hears me. I can't see where Rick has gone. He must be somewhere inside this vast closet. "I'm all set."

His head pops up on the other side of the nearest rack. "I'm ready too."

"Let's go."

He sweeps his heated gaze over me, and his voice drops to a softer, hungrier tone. "You are stunning, Maddie. Every time I see you in a new outfit, I'm awestruck again by how beautiful and sexy you are."

My cheeks warm from his compliment. I can't remember the last time I blushed because a man told me I'm beautiful, but I like the way it feels. I like him, a lot more than I expected I would. And I can't wait to swim in the nude with Richard Hunter.

I hustle around the rack between us so I can get a look at what he's wearing.

He's chosen the tiniest, tightest pair of swim briefs I have ever seen, even skimpier than the ones he'd worn on the day we met. When my attention lands on the bulge of his cock, I swear my mouth literally waters. I want to eat him up from head to toe and then do it all over again, licking and nibbling my way over every inch of his body.

Rick offers me his arm, like a true gentleman. "Shall we go?"

I finally notice he's wearing flip-flops too and a pair of sunglasses. "Yes, let's get a move on. I want to dive into that crystal-clear blue water with you. Like, right now. So hurry up, huh?"

Since I grin when I say that bossy part, he knows I'm teasing. But I'm sure he also realizes I do want to dive into the water with him—naked.

He snags a big umbrella, two big towels, and a bottle of sunscreen on our way out of the ginormous closet. I grab sunglasses for me and take the stuff he's carrying too so he can haul an armload of snorkeling fins and masks. He also picks up funny-looking little thingies that he tells me are earpieces to let us communicate while we're underwater.

A few minutes later, we're on the beach. Rick has laid out our towels, side by side, and jammed the umbrella's pole into the sand so the little canopy shades our towels. Palm trees surround us, and the scent of tropical flowers drifts on the breeze. The air always smells so nice in the Caribbean. Dr. Solberg scolds me for being unscientific in my analysis of the air, but I tell that girl to shut her mouth. This is my vacation. Screw the scientific method.

Rick holds up the sunscreen bottle. "Why don't I put some of this on you? Don't want all that beautiful skin to get burnt."

His smirk suggests he's less concerned about sunburn than about feeling me up from head to toe. I want that too, especially if it leads to more hot sex. But that will only happen if I can prove to him that I'm not sore.

I lie down on a towel on my stomach, propped up on my elbows, and glance at him over my shoulder. "I'm ready for that rubdown."

"Not a rubdown. It's a necessary application of sun protection." He's smirking again, so I figure he's being sardonic. He's definitely teasing me with that hot voice of his. "If you get aroused by this, it's not my fault."

"Uh-huh. Do you want me to sign a waiver? If I get hot and bothered, I absolve you of any and all responsibility for making me wet. Something like that?"

He stares at me from behind his reflective sunglasses. I can't see his eyes, but the fact he's staring is obvious, at least to me. I swear I can feel his sultry gaze on my skin. My scientist side, that annoying Dr. Solberg, balks at my claim. *Shut up, Doc. Maddie is enjoying her vacay and doesn't need your input.*

"Should I draft that waiver for you?" I ask.

"No." He kneels beside me and squeezes the sunscreen bottle, drizzling the cream onto my skin, painting a cool trail down my spine. "I like you wet, Maddie."

"But we agreed not to have sex."

With both palms, he rubs the sunscreen into my skin, spreading it all over, his hands warm and strong but his strokes gentle. "I want to make love to you again, believe me."

"Good. I want that too." I moan softly because his hands feel wonderful on my skin. "If you ever give up on publishing, you could have a solid career as a masseur. You'd have a line three blocks long full of women clamoring to get your hands on them."

He stops moving his fingers. When I glance back at him, he's scrunching his lips.

"Everything okay?" I ask.

"Yes, fine. Not a fan of professional massage, that's all." He goes back to rubbing that sunscreen all over me. "I appreciate the career advice, but I don't need a crowd of females. The only woman I want to get my hands on is you."

While he slides his palms up to my shoulders, I lay my head down on my clasped hands and close my eyes. Everything he does to me feels incredible. And I'm on vacation, so why shouldn't I revel in the pleasure of a sexy man massaging me all over?

For once, Dr. Solberg and I agree.

Chapter Sixteen

Richard

I couldn't pass up the chance to rub my hands all over Maddie's sensual body. The bikini she chose today is even sexier than the one she'd been wearing on the day we met. Was that only two days ago? I've lost count of the hours, the days, and everything else since I first saw her. I plan to relish every moment with her, in the moment, and let the future sort itself.

When I squeeze more sunscreen out of the bottle, letting it drizzle onto her shoulder, she shivers faintly.

"Too cold?" I ask.

"No, that's not why I shivered."

"Why, then?"

She opens one eye to look at me. "Because I'm turned on. Duh."

"Oh, I see." I'm getting turned on too, by the look on her face and the feel of her skin. "Would you rather do this yourself?"

"No, I'd rather you do it."

The husky tone of her voice makes me want to shag her right here, right now. But I can't. Not having sex for a while was my idea and reversing that decision would be…impolite. Or something like that.

"Keep going," she murmurs in that arousing tone. "Please."

I wonder if she could climax from a massage. Well, it probably depends on which parts of her I rub. My brother would know the perfect spots and the perfect ways to work them. No wonder women love him. Maybe that's why I haven't told Maddie about Nick yet. She wouldn't be the first woman to throw me over for my brother.

While I spread the sunscreen over her shoulders, I savor the sensation of her skin under my palms and the tendons I can feel when I knead her flesh with my fingers. She moans when I glide my hands down her back, skimming them over her arse on my way to her legs. I drizzle sunscreen onto her thighs and start rubbing, my fingers slick and my thoughts anything but chaste. To have my hands on her luscious body but not make love to her is sheer torture—but the best sort.

"Mm, Rick, talk to me. I love your voice."

"Thank you?" No one has ever complimented the way I speak. Is it a compliment? Yes, it must be.

She peeks at me over her shoulder, eyes half-closed. "Once, I tasted hot cocoa flavored with dark chocolate, caramel, and cayenne. Your voice is like that. Rich, smooth, decadent, and spicy."

I freeze with my hands on her thighs. What am I meant to say to that? She loves my voice, and it's like spicy hot cocoa. I have never heard that from any other woman.

Maddie smiles and wiggles her arse. "Are you done with my legs?"

"Not quite." I smooth the lotion onto her calves. "There. It's done."

"Time to turn over." She flips onto her back, clasping her hands behind her head. "I'm ready to get sunscreened up on the front side."

I can't resist doing what she wants, not when I'm enraptured by the sight of her breasts and her flat belly, with that sweet little navel that I'd love to tease with my tongue. Since I can't say no to this woman, I squeeze more lotion from the sunscreen bottle.

"Come on, Rick, please. Talk to me."

"All right." What should I say? While I slather the lotion over her skin, rubbing as I go, I realize I want to talk to her. Words tumble out of me, things I've never said to a woman before. "You are so fucking beautiful, Madeleine. I love touching you, and I love the look on your face when I'm touching your body. Christ, you're perfect. I want to tear off your bikini and devour every inch of you, starting with your breasts and moving lower and lower until I push my head between your thighs and feast on all that rich, luscious cream."

"Oh God, yes." Her chest rises and falls with every labored breath, hoisting those succulent tits. She drags her fingers down her throat and chest until she reaches her breasts. Then with only her fingertips, she toys with her nipples through her bikini top. "Keep talking."

If I do that, I know I'll wind up breaking my vow to not fuck her. Since my brain is on holiday, I can't quite remember why I shouldn't rip that bikini to shreds. But no sex was my idea. What sort of arse would I be if I changed my mind the day after making that vow?

I quickly finish applying the sunscreen, then I get up and rush to cover myself with it too—before she can offer to do it for me. My willpower will crumble to dust if she does that. But we can still have fun together, even without sex.

"Let's go snorkeling in the nude," she says. "I memorized all the fish and stuff that we might see down there so I'll know what to look for."

"You memorized the fish?"

Maddie hunches her shoulders, shifting her gaze downward. "I'm a scientist. Data is what I live for. So I bought books about Caribbean wildlife and sea life before I got on the plane. The long flight from the UK gave me plenty of time to commit all that info to memory."

"That's impressive. You're the cleverest woman I've ever met." I offer her my hands to help her up. "If we use the earpieces, you can tell me all about the fish we see."

She grins and claps her hands.

And my pulse speeds up. Maddie Solberg makes me feel…I don't know. Something good but indescribable. Maybe I'll figure out what it is later. For now, I want to watch her experience a coral-reef eco-system, because I'm certain she will light up when she swims with all those underwater creatures.

"I love your enthusiasm," I say. "But you're not at all what I thought a scientist would be like."

"How are we eggheads supposed to behave?"

"Serious and pragmatic, I suppose."

"That's how I am at work, but this is a vacation." She tickles my belly. "I'm serious about wanting to snorkel with you and doing it in the nude is very pragmatic."

"I don't see how."

"Hydrodynamics. It's like aerodynamics but in the water. I briefly dated a guy who specializes in that field, so I learned a few things about it. Swimming nude is practical because it means we'll have no clothes to slow down our hydrokinetic motion."

"Your gorgeous breasts are going to cock that up either way, I think." I pull her closer. "Not that I mind losing some hydro… whatever. It's worth it to see your naked body underwater."

"Are you agreeing to nude snorkeling?"

"Yes, you've convinced me. Strip, Maddie."

"Only if you do the same."

We both shed our swimsuits and apply sunscreen to the places our clothing had concealed, though we each do that on our own. Touching her naked body again would be too much temptation. Once we're both ready, I can't resist doing the same thing I'd done yesterday. I sweep her into my arms, carry her into the water until it's up to my knees, and toss her in.

Maddie shrieks and giggles and then splashes me. She grins again when she points behind me. "You forgot the snorkeling gear."

While I retrieve our fins and masks, a revelation hits me so powerfully that I freeze, bent over as I reach for our gear. Since we left our room this morning, I haven't thought about work once. Not even a fleeting thought.

Maddie races out of the water, grabbing her mask and fins from me. Her smile, so bright and exuberant, makes me smile too.

I haven't thought about work at all, and I plan to keep that up until the day I have no choice but to think about it. Work doesn't matter as much to me as it did a few days ago, and that's all thanks to one source.

Madeleine Louisa Solberg.

Chapter Seventeen

Maddie

*N*ude snorkeling is strange and wonderful, like we're doing something naughty, though there's nobody else around to object. Even if Dexter or Ilsa should see us, I doubt cither of thcm would takc offcnsc. Ycah, Dcx absolutcly would not mind. I bet he'd want to join us.

With these fancy earpieces and our full-face masks, Rick and I can talk to each other while underwater, so I tell him the names of the fish and other sea life. He seems genuinely excited to see and learn about all of it. We float a few feet above the reef where coral grows in shades of pink, yellow, orange, and green, and it grows in various shapes too, everything from brain coral that resembles the exterior of a human brain to bulbous forms, featherlike structures, rods, and tubular designs. I marvel at the diversity of coral, but the array of sea creatures swimming around and below us leaves me awestruck.

"This is unbelievable," Rick says in my earpiece. "What are all those fish?"

I point to each one as I tell him the names—a school of clown triggerfish with their white-spotted black bodies and bright-yellow mouths, and a queen angelfish with its blue-and-yellow body and rainbow-colored fins. When a fish with leopard-like spots passes below us, I point at the creature. "Look, it's a spotfin burrfish. Oh! Look at that over there. It's lavender rope sponge. That's the actual name of it, not just what it resembles. Isn't it beautiful?"

"It's lovely but not as beautiful as your arse."

I glance over my shoulder at him. He's slowed his swimming pace, apparently so he can admire my bottom. "You're supposed to be experiencing the beauty and majesty of the sea, Richard."

He swims closer so he can pat my rump. "I am doing that, but your arse is one of the great wonders of the sea and the entire world. You're surrounded by blue water and strange sea creatures, like a sexy mermaid prowling for men to seduce and drag down to your undersea kingdom."

"That's the weirdest compliment I've ever received."

"You deserve unique praise since you are a unique woman." He looks down, then points toward something below him. "What is that?"

"It's a green turtle. Isn't he gorgeous?"

"Yes, but I still think your arse is the most stunning sight."

Jeez, he's obsessed with my butt. Well, we are snorkeling in the nude, so I guess I should cut him some slack. I keep glancing at his nakedness too, especially the way his dick moves with the current of our movements.

We swim around for a while, but I don't try to gauge how much time has passed. It doesn't matter. We're both on vacation, with all our responsibilities and worries left behind. I haven't thought about disease and death at all since I came to the Caribbean and met Richard, except when I told him about my job. I've allowed myself to revel in the freedom of doing whatever I want, whenever I want, without suffering any guilt.

A manatee swims by below us, and I point it out to Rick. He's so excited about the sea life, which he tells me he's never seen in person before.

"Only a few fish," he admits, "that's all I ever saw."

I love being the one to show him this underwater kingdom, and I love his enthusiasm for every living thing we come across during our snorkeling adventure. He seems younger today like he's shed his worries and inhibitions along with his clothes.

We bob out of the water not far from shore, pulling our masks up so we can look at each other.

"Fun, huh?" I say.

"Bloody wonderful." He pulls me close with an arm around my waist. "I'm having the best time of my life, and that's because of you. Thank you, Maddie."

"You're welcome. I'm having a good time too, because you're here with me."

"I wouldn't want to be anywhere else."

Movement catches my eye peripherally, and I glance in that direction.

"Look!" I say, smacking Rick's arm to get his attention. "It's a dolphin!"

He swerves his head toward where I'm pointing just as the dolphin surges out of the water again, only to dive under the surface. "Bloody brilliant! I've never seen a dolphin before."

"Aren't they amazing? So graceful and pretty."

The dolphin pops up again and makes clicking sounds, then it vanishes into the blue water.

I shriek. Seriously, I do. For the first time in my life, I've seen a dolphin—and it's not more than thirty feet away. My pulse races, which seems dumb, but I can't help the giddiness that overtakes me at this moment, here in the crystalline aqua sea surrounded by beautiful, enchanting creatures and accompanied by a gorgeous, sweet, amazing man.

Once the dolphin swims away, we paddle back to shore and dry off with our towels, then we race back to the house while naked—and while carrying all our gear. Our footsteps slap on the bare floors inside the house as we sprint down the hall to the wardrobe room, laughing the whole time. Rick tickles me while I'm trying to get dressed, so I tickle him back. Turns out he's super ticklish on his chest, especially his nipples.

I love learning that about him.

And he learns where I'm the most ticklish—at the base of my spine, right above my buttocks.

For the next week, we have lots and lots of fun. More snorkeling, with and without swimsuits, and even some scuba diving. Dexter teaches us how to do that, and he and Ilsa join us for a magical dive into the deeper water farther from shore, where we see all kinds of mind-boggling creatures. Dex is far more knowledgeable about the sea life than I am, and he explains all of it with far more flair. That's not surprising since he's a writer, but his enthusiasm for all of it does surprise me. When we'd first met, I kind of dismissed Dex as a shameless flirt and a bit of a libertine, but I've come to appreciate his kindness, humor, and intelligence.

Every night before we go to sleep, Rick and I curl up in our big bed so I can read Dexter's book to him. Okay, it's not exactly Nobel Prize material, but I find myself getting interested in the bizarre behavior of the main character. Though I've never read or even heard of carnivalesque erotica before, I have fun reading the salacious text to Richard. He enjoys it too, and his nightly erections prove the sex scenes arouse him, but we haven't done the deed lately. Though I've fully recovered from my soreness, after spending each day exploring the island and the sea, we're too wiped out to do anything but sleep. It's the best kind of exhaustion, though, and I wouldn't trade this time with him for anything.

I've also discovered I love sharing a bed with Rick. We spoon, and I snuggle my backside against him. Often, we talk before we try to go to sleep.

One night, he asks me about my sister and my parents, whether we all get along.

"Sure, we get along great," I say. "Rika and I haven't been best friends, but we're getting closer these days. It's hard to forge strong relationships with anyone when I've been bouncing around the world for years, to places where cell phones don't work and nobody has a landline. Ham radio and satellite phones are the only means of communication."

"That must be difficult, being out of touch with your family. I've met Rika, and she talks about you all the time. I met your parents once, but we didn't get to talk much. That was at the engagement party for Dane and Rika."

"I've stayed with Rika and Dane a few times, but only for short visits. I wanted to spend more time with my sister, but work kept getting in the way. The last time I saw those two, they shipped me off to the Caribbean six days after I landed in England."

Rick has his body molded to mine, his chin on my shoulder and his arm draped over my midsection. He swirls his fingertips on my belly in a lazy motion. "Now we both know why Dane and Rika did that. They were playing matchmaker."

"You mean they were interfering in our lives." I lay my hand over his on my belly. "But I'm glad they did that. I love this vacation, especially since I met you."

"I love it too." He kisses my neck. "Meeting you is the best thing that's ever happened to me."

His statement makes my tummy flutter but also triggers an odd anxiety. I'm the best thing that's ever happened to him? I don't want to read too much into that, because maybe he means he loves having company, not that he's claiming to have feelings for me. The mix of anxiety and excitement sparked by his statement suggests I might have feelings for him. Even if that's true, I can't think about it right now. We've known each other for a week. Dr. Solberg whispers in my head that I cannot fall for a man after such a short time, but Maddie wants to dive in and drown in the rush of it all.

Meeting Richard Hunter has changed my life in ways I can't even explain yet. Coming to the Caribbean, and especially to Dexter's private island, has also changed me. In a week, I have to fly back to England and figure out what on earth to do with myself now. Should I accept Naveen's offer to work at the CDC? For the next week, I vow not to worry about any of that. I want to know Rick better and find out if we could have something more than fantastic sex, if we mean something to each other beyond a friend to share new experiences with.

And I know what I need to do to find those answers. I need to interrogate him.

In the morning. Tonight, all I want is to fall asleep in his arms.

Chapter Eighteen

Richard

For the first time since I met Maddie, she's already awake when I rouse from the best night's sleep I've ever had. The more time I spend with her, the more relaxed I feel. So it's no surprise to me that I sleep better too. Having her body tucked against mine while we both drift off plays a large part in that. I even love listening to her snore. It's always soft little snorts, nothing that would keep me awake all night, and it's only the occasional bout of snoring.

I sometimes wake up overnight to see her smiling in her sleep. Is she dreaming about me? I dream about her every night.

This morning, she's lying on her side next to me when I open my eyes and yawn.

Maddie tickles my chest, which I unfortunately let her find out is the only place on my body where I am ticklish. I manage to hold back my laughter—until she tickles my nipple.

She laughs too.

I can't resist fluttering my lips over her belly, which always makes her giggle. Since she's facing me, I can't reach her most ticklish spot, that area in the middle of her back just above her arse.

"Cut that out," she says while still laughing and while I'm still teasing her belly with my lips. "My eyes are starting to water."

"All right. I suppose I have to stop." I've never been the sort who tickles a woman's belly, but with Maddie, I can't resist doing that. Her laughter is more intoxicating than cognac.

She rolls onto her back and stretches, yawning again. "Do you have any brothers or sisters? We've talked about my family, but you haven't said much about yours."

I rub my jaw and sigh. I don't want to talk about my brother. I love him, but discussing Nick brings up an issue I'd rather not share with Maddie yet. Maybe never. Of course, "never" would mean I can't introduce her to him, and I want her to meet my family. She's gazing at me with curiosity in her eyes, and I know the sexy scientist lying beside me needs the facts. I can leave out one or two of them, though, can't I? Omission isn't exactly lying.

"Uh, yes, I have a brother," I say. "We're very different sorts, but we do have a good relationship. I have to admit, I've never understood his career choice. It's…strange."

"What does he do?"

"Nicholas is a massage therapist."

She tries to stifle a laugh, but only half succeeds. "What's bizarre about that?"

"Most of his clients are women, which makes the whole thing bizarre, at least to me. Touching strange, naked women all day long?" I shake my head. "Can't imagine doing that for a living. Once word got round that Nick Hunter opened a massage business, they started flocking to him."

"Wait. Your names are Rick and Nick? Like you're twins or something?" She taps her finger on my lips. "Let me guess. He's as hot as you are."

"I suppose so." Do I sound uneasy when I say that? Probably. Time to steer the subject away from Nick. "As for my parents, I have a very good relationship with them."

"That's nice. I always feel bad for people who don't get along with their families. My parents and my sister are wonderful, and we all support each other however we can."

"It's the same with my family. The Dixons are like that too."

"Have you met Alex Thorne?"

"Yes, I know him. He's the strangest man I've ever met."

"He's unusual, for sure." She drums her fingers on her belly while she gets that serious-thoughts look on her face. "Why do the Dixons call him their cousin? They realized not long after they met him that he's not a blood relative. Alex's half-brother is their cousin."

"Blood isn't everything. When Alex was a boy, a sweet couple adopted him and raised him as their son. He calls them Mum and Dad, but they're not biologically related."

"That's true. Guess I need to broaden my idea of family beyond the scientific definition." She blows out a sigh. "Anyway, Alex is quite a character. It's weird how all you Brits have the same smooth voices. Must be something in the water over there."

"Maybe American water is laced with hallucinogens."

"Oh please. This is factual, not the result of an acid trip. You sound surprisingly like your British pals."

"What about Dexter?" I ask. "He's British too. I hope you're not suggesting I sound like him."

"He's older and wickeder, but yeah. Your voices are kind of similar."

"What are you implying? It's not like we all sound identical, as if our voices are being narrated by one bloke."

She gives my chest a halfhearted shove. "Ha-ha, go ahead and make fun of me. If I can handle interviewing drug runners just so I can pinpoint the source of a disease outbreak, I can handle your scorn."

"It's not scorn. I love the barmy things you say. But for the record, I do *not* sound like Dexter or Alex Thorne."

"Shouldn't a publisher have a thicker skin? I mean, you must reject people all the time."

"Let's not talk about work or other men's voices while we're naked in bed together." I kiss a trail up her throat and nuzzle her ear. "I'd much rather talk about you, Maddie. You're an extraordinary woman. You confront criminals, memorize an entire catalog of fish species, handle a randy old goat with ease, and have a deep passion for everything you do."

"If you don't stop paying me compliments, I might start to blush."

"Then I won't stop. I love seeing you blush." I still have my face against her cheek and ear, so I slip my tongue out to tease her lobe. "I love everything about you."

"I like you lots too," she murmurs, turning her face toward me, her lips grazing mine. "I know we agreed to wait to have sex, but the timeline was vague. 'A few days,' you said. Seems like it's been more than that."

"Are you still sore?"

"Nope."

"Then let's do it."

She grins. "Seriously?"

"Yes." I skim a hand up and down her arm. "I will make love to you, Maddie, but after breakfast. Dexter invited us to join him in the dining room this morning, remember? Besides, I need to bite that bullet and talk to Dex about his book."

"Sure, I can wait a couple more hours." She catches my bottom lip between her teeth, flicks her tongue across it, and lets it go. "You're not fooling me. You don't hate Dex's book. I know because you get a hard-on every time I read it to you."

"That's because *you* are reading it. Your voice does that to me. I should hire you to narrate audiobooks for my company."

"No, it's you and your friends who should do that."

"Me?" I laugh. "I'd be awful at it."

She sits up, stretching and smiling. "Wouldn't it be weird if we did have narrators performing every word we say, like we're puppets? I think I saw a movie like that once. Whatever an author wrote, some guy heard it in his head like an audiobook."

"That's rubbish," I say, shaking my head while I struggle not to laugh. "You're having me on, aren't you? I sound nothing like Alex Thorne or the Dixons. And I certainly don't have an author in my head writing every word I say."

She kisses me. "Okay, no more teasing you about your voice. You're kind of sensitive about that, aren't you?"

"No, I'm not." I slide off the bed, and the cold wood floor chills my feet. "Think I'll have a shower before breakfast."

"Do we have time for that?"

"Ilsa stopped by last night while you were snoring to let us know breakfast will be served at eight o'clock. It's only half seven."

"Think I'll call my sister while you're getting clean. Rika's been texting me for days, but I ignored her." She sweeps her gaze over my entire body. "Maybe you shouldn't take a shower. I love it when you're dirty."

"Sweat-encrusted isn't sexy."

"You might have a point there." She pinches her nostrils between her thumb and forefinger while waving the other hand as if she's trying to eradicate a bad smell. "Whew, do you stink."

I latch an arm around her waist and drag her closer, then I crouch so I can plant my mouth on her belly and blow, making my lips vibrate on her skin. She giggles. I keep doing that, moving my mouth around until I find a spot that makes her shriek with laughter. Only when I notice her eyes are watering do I stop.

"Now, let's try that again," I say. "How do I smell?"

She wipes her eyes with her fingers. "That was a dirty trick."

"But you like me dirty. You just said so."

"Yep, I did."

"And the correct answer to my question is…"

She grins again. "You smell wonderful."

I slap her arse and head for the bathroom.

Maddie claims I sound like my mates, which is bollocks. But it makes me wonder, or maybe this is worry I'm feeling. What will she think when she meets Nick?

Chapter Nineteen

Maddie

I get dressed, then I sprawl on the bed and call Rika. She's in the UK, so the time difference means it's afternoon over there. I know I shouldn't have ignored all her texts, but I had other things on my mind. Well, one other thing. Richard Hunter has taken my mind off everything else for more than a week, and though it's been bliss, I can't avoid real life forever.

"What have you been doing?" Rika asks as soon as she picks up, not even waiting for me to say hello. "Please tell me you've ignored my calls and texts because you're having a steamy fling with a guy you met at the resort."

"Like you don't already know the answer to that. You and Dane conspired to commit felony matchmaking. I should have you both arrested."

"Did you hook up with Richard Hunter? Dane didn't believe our plan would work, but I told him to have faith in the power of destiny."

"What a load of bullshit. Destiny? You and your husband maneuvered me into a Caribbean vacation because you knew Richard would be here."

"Sure, we did that. But we couldn't make you fall for him."

I make a rude noise. "Who says I'm falling for him? I met Rick last week."

"Rick?" My sister now sounds way too pleased with herself. "He only lets people call him that if he really likes them. We might've steered you two into each other's orbits, but we couldn't manufacture chemistry."

"I like Richard. That's all."

"Have you slept with him?"

"None of your business, Rika."

"Oh, you must have it bad." She pauses, then adds in a sneaky tone, "Should I start planning the wedding?"

"You are so annoying. Do I ask if you're sleeping with Dane?"

My sister laughs. "I'm married to him. Of course we have sex. But you and Richard Hunter…"

"Are not soul mates or whatever unscientific hooey you're thinking of. We're getting to know each other, period. Do *not* start planning the wedding."

"If it was love at first sight, you'd deny it. For once, please don't get all scientific. Let yourself be free."

"No more talking about Richard. Okay? Tell me what you've been up to."

Rika tells me more about the Dixon boys and their cousin Grey, not to mention Grey's brother Alex, and then she recounts their recent adventures. I've met all those guys, but Rika knows the details I've missed out on. Chance, Dane, and Reese have known their cousin Grey all their lives, but Alex Thorne is new to the family—though like I told Rick, Alex isn't technically their family. They've decided he's their cousin anyway, despite the fact he's not a blood relation. After my brief discussion with Rick about that issue, I realize he's right that blood isn't everything. Feelings can't be quantified or explained by the scientific method. I've learned that lesson since I met Richard Hunter. Sometimes you have to do what feels right, even if it makes no sense. The heart has its own logic.

I listen while Rika goes on and on about Dane—how sweet he is, how brilliant he is, what an amazing lover he is, et cetera. Thankfully, she keeps the sex details to herself. I don't mind hearing all that stuff. I love my sister, and knowing she found the right guy makes me happy too.

"Don't get all analytical about it," Rika says when she finally stops gushing about Dane.

"Analytical about what?"

"Your feelings for Richard." She speaks slowly like I'm a child who won't understand otherwise. "You like him. Don't overthink it."

"Fine, I promise not to think too much." Or at all. Whenever I'm with Rick, I don't use my brain much. My libido takes control. But lately, another part of me vies for control too—my heart, which I plan to follow no matter how crazy its advice is.

"Just think," Rika says, "you might wind up married to a multimillionaire."

"What are you talking about?"

"Richard. He's got millions in the bank. Everybody knows that."

"Not me. I mean, I figured he had money, but not multimillions." Holy moly, that's a lot of zeroes on his bank statement. "Doesn't matter to me. I like him because he's a good man, not because he's stinking rich. And in case you plugged your ears when I said it before, do not start planning the wedding."

"Oh, fine. Have it your way. I'll wait until you guys get back from your vacation."

I give up on reining in my sarcastic sister, and Rika and I say goodbye just as Richard saunters out of the bathroom.

He's naked. Though he's dried off his body, his hair is still wet.

That man looks even hotter wet and naked, fresh from a shower.

I jump off the bed and walk up to him, splaying my palms on his chest. "I love it when you're damp. It's almost as sexy as when you're dripping wet after a swim."

He links his hands behind my back, tugging me closer. "I love it when you're dripping wet too, and I'm not only talking about when we swim in the sea."

I love it when I'm wet for him too, and that's happening right now.

But we agreed to have breakfast with Dexter. *Rats.*

Rick gets dressed, to my severe disappointment, and we amble downstairs hand in hand. When we get to the dining room, we find our host sitting at the head of the long table, sipping what looks like a mimosa. Is that a real one with champagne? I'd love one of those.

"Good morning, lovebirds," Dex says with a smile. "Have a seat. Breakfast will be served at any moment."

Rick pulls out a chair for me, the one right beside Dexter, and I settle into it. Then Rick starts to walk around the table, apparently to take the chair beside Dex on the opposite side of the table.

Our host holds up a hand. "No, Rick, sit beside Madeleine. You can't fondle her under the table if you're on the other side of it. Unless Maddie wants me to take over that duty."

"She doesn't want that," Richard says as he sits down in the chair beside me. "Your devil-goat horns are showing, Dex."

"I've never tried to hide my horns. Why should I? Women love them."

The gray-haired woman who always brings us dinner pushes a wheeled cart into the dining room. She sets plates full of food in front of us, along with two mimosas—one for me, and one for Richard.

I take a sip and realize I'd been right. The mimosas do have champagne in them this morning. The bubbly liquid tickles my throat, and I love it. But I absolutely will not overindulge today.

Dex makes a toast, and we all clink our glasses.

Throughout breakfast, we chat and laugh. Dexter is a lot of fun to talk to, but I'd rather be alone with Rick. Our private conversations are the most fun, even when we don't engage in sex of any kind. I love spending time with him, period.

Once the meal is over, Richard asks Dexter if they can talk business now. Dexter agrees but suggests the sitting room might be a better place for that. He leads us down the hall and into that room, then offers us cognac. I decline because, jeez, it's morning—not late night at a bar that's offering half-price cocktails for all the lushes. Mimosas are one thing. Cognac is a whole other universe, one where I will get myself into trouble again for sure. I decline Dex's offer, and so does Rick. We take the little sofa while Dex relaxes in his big chair.

He sighs. "All right. Let's talk business, if we must."

"We must," Rick says. He tugs at the collar of his T-shirt, twisting his lips this way and that. "I need to talk to you about your, ah, book."

"Do you? I've been wondering how long it would take you to get round to that." Dexter glances at me and wags his eyebrows. "Then again, you've had the most splendid distraction in the world."

Rick clears his throat, twice. "About the book..."

"Spit it out, man. I might expire while I wait for you to speak."

"The story is certainly titillating, but I—"

A phone rings. A cell phone, I assume, since the ringing seems to originate in Dexter's pants. He holds up a finger, silently asking us to wait, then extricates the phone from his pocket and answers. "Hello, lovey, what are you wearing?"

Richard's brows hike up, and he glances sideways at me.

I shrug.

He sinks back into the sofa, rubbing his forehead.

Dexter chuckles. "Yes, lovey, we can do that later. You know how I love to watch you get your kit off, even if it is only a virtual striptease. Yes, I know you'll actually undress, but from my end, it's a virtual experience."

He chuckles, then says goodbye to whoever's on the other end of the call.

"A virtual striptease?" I ask. "Dexter, you are such a naughty man."

"The naughtiest." Our host gives me a sly smile. "If I ask nicely, would you treat me to an in-person striptease?"

"No, she won't," Rick announces.

A smile tugs at my lips. "Maybe another time, Dex."

Rick stares at me, his brows rising so high I think they might join up with his hairline.

"That was a joke," I say, nudging him with my shoulder.

"Of course it was," Dexter says. "I love to tease everyone. Now, about the book."

Rick looks at me, his lips tight, his face pinched.

I lay a hand on his thigh. "Just be honest. Dex will appreciate that, I'm sure."

"Yes," our host says, "I always value honesty. Spit it out, man."

Rick shuts his eyes briefly, his posture sagging, then he meets Dexter's gaze. "The book is utter rubbish. I can't publish it."

Chapter Twenty

Richard

I watch Dexter's facial expression but can't tell anything from it, so I have no idea how my bald announcement affects him. He seems…not impassive, but sort of unperturbed. Maddie clasps my hand. I want to look at her, but I feel like I should keep my focus on Dexter until he responds. I owe him that much, don't I? To behave like a professional instead of like a nervous moron who can't maintain eye contact. Dex has let us stay in his home and has welcomed us like family.

All right, I like Dexter. He's what I imagine my grandfather might be like if he suddenly developed an insatiable lust for women, drink, and risqué humor. My real grandfather is nothing like that, though they do share certain traits. They're kind gents who might be elderly in terms of age, but in temperament, they're as young as anyone.

Dexter braces an elbow on his chair's arm, bending his head to rub his chin while he regards me with an unreadable expression. "Are you sure you don't want to publish it?"

"Yes, I'm sure. And I'm sorry about that, Dex, more than you can know."

He keeps rubbing his chin. His eyes narrow for a moment, then he straightens and smiles. "Jolly good! You wouldn't believe how long I've waited for someone to reject that book. Everyone I've offered it to has been thrilled to snap it up and give me a large advance. I declined their offers."

"You wanted me to reject the book?"

"Of course I did. It is, as you said, utter rubbish."

I rub my forehead, struggling to make sense of this conversation. "Was this all some sort of test?"

"Precisely. For all these years, I've kept writing. But I'd had my fill of smarmy publishers and agents who will release any old rot if they think it will sell or if the author will pay them to publish it. So I stopped submitting my books, and I rejected all attempts by those industry cretins to woo me back into their world." Dexter sighs, gazing down at the floor. "I thought I would never want to publish another book."

"But now you do," Maddie says. "That's why you contacted Richard."

"Correct. A year ago, I decided to dip my toes back into the industry's tepid waters. Ilsa helped me get the word out via social media posts that 'leaked' the secret information that the world's most reclusive author has a new book and is looking for a publisher."

"I wasn't the first person you contacted," I say. "How many agents and publishers did you invite to your private island?"

"Only you."

"But you just said—"

"You're making an incorrect inference. I said that a year ago I decided to leak the fact I have a new book, to attract offers for it. But I did not say I invited anyone to my home. They needed to pass my test first, and none of them did."

I slide forward on the sofa until I'm perched on the edge, while I try to understand any of this. "But you wouldn't even tell me what your book was about until I flew to the Caribbean. Then you kept putting me off, inviting me to meet with you only to cancel on me."

"That's the test. Well, part of it." Dexter slouches a touch in his chair, propping his feet on the coffee table between us. "None of the others made it past the first phone call. They were greedy and dishonest. I could tell as much from a five-minute conversation. Whenever I asked one of those morons if they wanted to know what the book is about, they would say they didn't need to know. If I wrote it, they'd publish it. No questions asked."

"Of course they didn't ask questions. You are the Holy Grail of publishing." I wince. "Sorry. That sounded ridiculous. I meant—"

"I know what you meant, and your honesty is refreshing. You are an ethical and honorable man, which is why I made you fly here all the way from the UK so I could give you the final test."

"Your test is that awful book."

"Precisely. I've sent sample chapters to a few agents, and they all told me it was brilliant, my next Nobel winner. It's bollocks. I know it, they know it, you and Maddie know it, everyone knows it." He drops his feet to the floor and leans forward to gaze intently at me. "You are the first one who has ever told me so. Thank you, Rick."

"I was only being honest."

"And that means a great deal to me." Dexter blows out a breath, slaps his hands on his thighs, and stands. "I think it's time I gave you the real books."

"Did you say books, plural?"

"That's right. I have eight of them to give you."

Eight never-before-published novels by Dexter Armstrong-Hill? That's more than the Holy Grail of publishing. It's like simultaneously finding the Holy Grail and Atlantis, winning every lottery on the planet, discovering the cure for every disease on earth, and cracking the code of immortality. All right, I might be blowing this out of all proportion. But for me, this is the most astonishing coup I've ever accomplished, for myself and my company.

Once I've recovered from the shock, I say, "Thank you for trusting me with your life's work, Dexter. It means a lot that you've chosen me to publish these books. Of course, I'll need to review them first."

I think I stop breathing while I wait for his response. Why am I nervous? Dexter chose me, so surely, he won't be offended that I need to read the novels before offering him a contract. I doubt anyone else would bother with that, and maybe I shouldn't either, but I need to do this the right way. I've made mistakes in the past, and I will not cock this up too.

Dexter leans across the table to offer me his hand. "It will be a pleasure to work with you, Mr. Hunter."

As we shake hands, I ask, "You're all right with me reading the books before we negotiate a contract?"

"Naturally, you'll need to read them. I never expected you wouldn't."

"You're an honorable man too, Dex. I'm sure you know how rare honor is in the publishing world."

"Indeed I do. I'll retrieve those manuscripts for you."

He leaves us alone in the sitting room.

Maddie throws her arms around me, showering my face with kisses. "Congratulations, Rick. You did it. You won over the most elusive author in the world, and he's giving you *eight* books. I'm so proud of you."

"Proud?" I can't help chuckling, even while she keeps peppering my forehead with soft, quick kisses. "We've only just met. How do you know I'm not lying through my teeth to get Dex to hand over his precious manuscripts?"

"You wouldn't do that." She pulls away, but only enough that we can look at each other. Her hands rest on my shoulders, and she aims her loving gaze straight into mine. "Maybe I haven't known you for very long, but like I told you last week, I can gauge someone's character pretty fast. You are a good man. Dexter is lucky to have you in his corner. So am I."

I can't speak. Her declaration might be the sweetest thing anyone has ever said to me. This incredible woman believes in me. It seems insane considering we met last week, but I will not overanalyze this. Maddie makes me feel good in so many ways, and I never want to give that up.

Dexter comes back into the room carrying an armload of boxed manuscripts. He drops them onto the coffee table. "Here you are, mate. You might go cross-eyed after reading all of these, but I'm sure Maddie can help you relax afterward."

He winks at her.

She shakes her head, though her lips kick up at the corners. "Dex, you have the narrowest one-track mind ever."

"It's part of my charm." He taps a finger on the stack of manuscripts. "You will find sexual content in these stories, but nothing like that outrageous farce of a book I gave you last week."

"Thank you, Dex," I say. "Can't wait to read these."

"You and Madeleine are welcome to stay here for as long as you like."

"While I'd love to do that, I'll need to head back to the resort so I can communicate with my team in the UK and draft a contract. I need an internet connection for that."

"Of course," he says. "I do apologize for the wicked trick I played on you, and I'm chuffed that you passed the test."

"I'm extremely pleased too. And I understand you had reasons for testing me." I glance at Maddie. "Will you be going back to the resort with me? If you'd rather stay here…"

"No, I'm with you."

My mind can't help interpreting that statement as some sort of declaration of…what? Not love. We barely know each other. Affection? That makes more sense, and I feel affection for her too. In the brief time we've been together, I've come to care for her more than I've cared for anyone in a long time.

"I'll ring the helicopter service," Dex says, "and have you picked up as soon as possible."

"Thank you," I say. "I really am looking forward to reading your books."

And my gut instincts tell me I won't be disappointed. Have I saved my company? It's too early to claim that, but I know one thing for certain. I have been saved in other ways—by Madeleine Solberg.

Chapter Twenty-One

Maddie

An hour after Dexter handed over his books, Richard and I enter the lobby of the resort with the eight boxed manuscripts in our arms. I carry two while Rick carries six. He insisted on that since the boxes are kind of heavy. A bellboy took our suitcase, the one Dex had given us to carry the clothes he gifted to us from his private collection. That bag will be waiting for us in our suite.

Though I've been sleeping in the same bed with Rick for over a week, it still feels strange, in a good way, to think about sharing a suite with him.

We stop at the concierge desk to arrange for lunch to be sent to our room, then we hurry up to the fourth floor. The bellboy has already come and gone, and our shared suitcase waits for us just inside the door. The concierge promised our lunch would arrive in thirty minutes precisely.

"What should we do until the food comes?" I ask.

"I need to get started on reading these books." He sets his stack of boxes on the floor. "This might take weeks."

"Can I help?" I drop my two boxes on the bed. "I'm a fast reader, but I also have high reading comprehension even when I speed read."

"I have no doubts you do. You're the cleverest woman on earth."

"You keep saying things like that. I appreciate the compliments, but you don't need to go overboard."

"I'm not going overboard. You are the most remarkable woman, the most remarkable person, I've ever met." He slings an arm around my waist, pulling me close. "Your sister told me you save lives every day, and you told me how you confronted drug traffickers. Not only that, but you have stayed with me throughout this whole nonsense with Dexter. I would've given up days ago, but you convinced me to see it through to the end. You are more than remarkable, Maddie. You're a miracle."

My cheeks warm, despite the fact he's spouted another overblown compliment. I don't care. Everything he says about me makes me want to snuggle up with him forever. It's a little embarrassing to receive such extravagant compliments, but I know he means every word. "Thank you, Rick, but it's not like I'm a superhero. I do my job to the best of my ability, that's all. And I stay with you because I want to, because you make me feel so good."

"The feeling is mutual." He kisses my forehead, then steps back. "If you really want to help, let's each take a manuscript and start reading."

"You trust me to review books for you?"

"Absolutely."

I pick up a manuscript box. "Let's get started."

For the next half hour, we read while sitting side by side on the bed, our legs stretched out. When our lunch arrives, we take a short break to eat, but then it's back to the grindstone. It's hardly a chore reading Dexter's writing. Though I'd loved his early books, this new one I've got in my hands is even better. The story has emotion, insight, and just enough steamy scenes to make me want to rip Richard's clothes off. I restrain myself, though, and keep reading. We take the occasional breather to relax and give each other neck rubs, and once we even take a swim in the infinity pool. We also order snacks—cupcakes, naturally, in a multitude of flavors—and feed each other like newlyweds, stuffing cupcakes into each other's mouths.

By evening, we've both finished our books.

Richard gets to the end first and watches me while I finish the manuscript I've been poring over all afternoon. The second I set down the last page, he speaks.

"How was it?"

"Wonderful," I say. "Even better than his earlier books. How was yours?"

"The best thing Dex has ever written. And his sex scenes make me so randy I've had a devil of a time keeping my hands off you."

"I have the solution to that problem." I dump the manuscript I've had on my lap onto the floor. While the pages spill across the wood, I climb onto Rick's lap and straddle him. "I'd love to have your hands all over me, not to mention the rest of you."

"There's no reason to hold back anymore, is there? We've had more than a week of getting to each know each other the celibate way." He grasps my hips, rocking them forward into his stiffening cock. "I want you, Maddie. Right now."

"I want you too."

He dumps his manuscript on the floor, where its pages spill out to mingle with the ones I tossed away a minute ago. "Strip for me, Madeleine."

As much as I love the way his voice sounds when he calls me Maddie, I get even wetter and hotter when he speaks my full name. "Are you asking me to do a striptease for you?"

"Yes." He glances out at the aqua waters of the bay. "Maybe we should move outdoors. I'd love to shag you on the beach in the moonlight. We can go back to that secluded spot where I first kissed you."

"I'd love that. Let's go."

We both slip sandals on, but we leave our cell phones in the room. Rick snags a handful of condoms from a drawer in the bedside table. I don't make any snarky comments about how many condoms he's bringing along, because I need him to make love to me several times. It's been too long since I've felt him inside me.

Rick grabs a picnic blanket and ushers me out of the suite. The elevator ride seems to take forever, and there are other people in here with us, so we can't make out. At last, we escape the hotel and run to the beach. A small group of revelers is there, gathered around a bonfire, but we hurry past them to our favorite spot where we can have some privacy. Well, as much privacy as two people can get on a beach at a busy resort. I don't care if anyone finds us while we're having sex. Maybe I would have cared a couple of weeks ago, but today, I don't mind at all.

Once we reach our favorite spot, Rick spreads the blanket out and sits down. "Strip for me, Maddie."

Warmth sweeps over my skin, awakening all those secret places where I know he'll touch me and stroke me to drive me wild. I position myself near his feet, a yard or so away to make sure he can see all of me while I do this for him. No man has ever asked me to give him a striptease. Most guys can't wait to get me naked, but for their own pleasure, not mine. Get naked, screw, fall asleep. That's it. But Richard Hunter wants more. He always has, even that first night when we didn't know each other's names.

Luckily, I'm wearing shorts and a button-up blouse, plus under-wear, so I have plenty of material to drive him as wild as he makes me feel. I'd kicked off my sandals the second we got to the beach, so I'm ready to go.

Rick stretches out on the blanket and links his hands under his head, his hooded gaze trained on me.

God, I love it when he looks at me that way.

I take hold of the top button on my blouse and unhook it slowly, then I move on to the next button, and the one after that. My gaze is bound to his, and every time I free another but-ton, I swear the bulge in his pants gets bigger. When I unhook the last button, and my blouse falls open just enough to expose part of my tummy and my cleavage, he drags his tongue over his bottom lip. I push the blouse off one shoulder and bite my lip, letting it slide free of my teeth little by little. He shifts in place like his groin is paining him, but I know he's not suffering. I'm torturing him with my body, with my sensual striptease, and we both love it.

Pushing the blouse off my other shoulder, I trail my fingertips down the center of my chest until they bump into my bra. The sen-sation makes me shiver the tiniest bit, but only because of the way Rick is devouring me with his gaze. I roll my shoulders back and let the blouse fall away, fluttering to the floor.

He rubs his hands up and down his thighs like he's imagining doing that to my body.

I unbutton my shorts, then grasp the zipper pull.

Rick crooks his fingers into his thighs, making his pants bunch up under them. His attention zeroes in on my fingers and that tiny metal pull I grasp between them.

I sway my hips, tossing my hair, and tip my head back to expose my throat. While I dance for him, I drag that zipper down, down, down, millimeter by millimeter. Between my thighs, a silky heat gathers, and I burn and throb in ways that make my breaths shorten. I can't stop staring at his erection, concealed inside his pants, even while I push my shorts over my hips and let them tumble down to my ankles. With one kick, I get rid of them.

Rick unzips his pants and slips a hand inside to cup his cock.

"Don't go off without me," I say, wagging a finger at him.

"I won't. For over a week, the thought of shagging you again has tormented me. Nothing is going to keep me from fucking you the second you've gotten rid of your bra and knickers."

Oh yes, I want that. All these days without feeling him inside me have been a torment for me too. The best kind. The hot and steamy kind. This has been worth the wait, but I don't want to delay one second longer than necessary.

I unhook my bra and shrug to make the straps slip off my shoulders. The way I've crossed my arms under my breasts keeps the bra in place, and though I'd love to torture Richard some more, I can't wait that long. I peel the bra away from my breasts and toss it away, then I shimmy out of my panties.

He strips off his shirt and starts to wriggle out of his pants.

My gaze is glued to him, to what he's doing, while I drop to my hands and knees on the sand. I crawl toward him inch by inch, my hips and my breasts swaying. That movement catches his attention, and he gets tangled up in his pants while trying to kick them off, so obsessed with watching my tits that he's ignoring everything else.

"Bollocks!" he half hisses, half shouts, still struggling with his pants.

"Let me do it." I wave his hands away and free his legs, flinging his pants onto the floor. Then I crawl even closer, walking my hands up his chest while I straddle his lap. "All naked now. It's your move."

"Mine? I thought women liked to be in charge."

"Yeah, but I did my thing. My striptease got you crazed with lust." I bend my arms to bring my face closer to his. "Now it's your turn to make me crazy-hot for you."

"I'm already naked, so I can't do a striptease." He dips his head to capture my nipple, scraping his teeth over the tip while he suckles it. When I gasp, he pulls his mouth away just enough that he can speak. "You inspire me in every way imaginable."

"You do the same for me."

"Lie on your back, please."

I slide off his lap and settle in beside him on the blanket.

Rick turns on his side, facing me. For a moment, he just lies there drinking in the sight of me. "You have the most beautiful body I've ever seen, but I love your eyes most of all."

"I love your smile best." I skate my hand along his arm, helpless to resist squeezing his biceps. "But your body is what I need right now."

He gets a condom out of his pants pocket and covers himself. "Spread your legs for me, love."

Without a second's hesitation, I do it.

He kneels over me, placing one leg between both of mine, then lifts my leg onto his shoulder while he turns sideways, bracing his other arm on the blanket near my hip. My free leg is now wedged between his thighs, and when he pushes inside me oh-so-slowly, I feel every inch of him gliding in deeper and deeper until he can't go in any farther. When he starts to thrust in easy, measured strokes, I feel him even more. His body is rubbing against my clitoris like never before and the intensity of the sensations has me gasping and begging him to go even deeper. His biceps bulge from the effort of holding himself in this position, but he seems relaxed and focused on the task like it's no effort at all. God, that makes me want him even more. He's so strong, so agile, so adventurous and creative, all the things that make a man an incredible lover.

But the thing that makes me so hot for him that I can barely breathe isn't his physical strength or the way he's thrusting into me. It's the way he keeps his gaze trained on mine. I can't stop looking at him. The heat in his blue eyes burns into me, sizzling through my entire body, and I desperately want to grip his arms or his shoulders, but I can't reach him.

"Rick," I moan. "Come closer, please. I need to touch you."

He angles toward me, forcing my leg to bend backward, and suddenly I'm grateful for all those yoga classes I took. He tilts closer and closer, pushing my leg toward my chest while easing it slightly to the side to make room for his body. When he lowers his head, his mouth comes within an inch of mine. "Close enough?"

"Yes, thank you."

I grip his face with both hands and kiss him, plunging my tongue inside his mouth in strokes that match the pace of his cock plunging into my body. He groans deeply, the sound resonating in his chest and vibrating into me. He's rubbing into my stiff nub even more now, and he begins to thrust harder and faster, spurring me to push my tongue into his mouth harder and faster too.

He pries his lips away from mine. "God, Maddie, I—"

"Keep going, Rick, please. I'm so close."

My body is on fire from head to toe, but the blaze burns hottest deep inside where he's consuming me with strokes that grow wilder with every thrust. I grip his arms, arching my back, my mouth falling open though I can't make any sounds. Everything inside me tightens and readies for the climax that's about to rip me through me any second. I can't breathe, caught in that moment right before bliss hits, teetering on the edge for so long that my ears start to ring.

Rick pulls his hips back and punches into me, shouting my name.

And I sail off that precipice, free-falling into a mind-altering orgasm, sailing through outer space with my eyes squeezed shut while stars burst around me. Weightless, I soar through the emptiness, but I don't feel empty or alone, not with his length inside me and my body clenching his cock over and over. When he shouts my name again and slams into me one last time, the pleasure of feeling his release explode out of him makes me come even harder. It launches me into deep space, where nothing exists except the two of us joined in every way.

Once it's over, I float back down to earth. Sucking in a deep breath, I force myself to exhale it slowly. I keep doing that until the ringing in my ears fades. Rick is still inside me, still on top of me, but he has his face buried against my neck. His chest heaves, and his breaths bluster over my skin. He mumbles something, but it's muffled by my neck.

"Sorry, I didn't catch that," I say, running my hands over his back.

He lifts his head to look at me. "I said that was the best sex in the history of the world."

I laugh. "Best in history? Wow, I might need to put that on a bumper sticker. 'Maddie gives Richard the best orgasms since the dawn of time.' No, that won't work. It's too long to fit on a bumper sticker."

"Shorten it to 'Maddie plus Rick equals best shag ever.' That might fit." He pulls out of my body and rolls off me, though he slings an arm over me to hold me close. His chin rests on my shoulder. "I need to go home. Back to England."

That beautiful glow I've been enjoying since our simultaneous climaxes evaporates. He's leaving. I knew it would happen sooner or later, but I'd let myself forget it for all this time. My chest aches, but it's not a heart condition. Well, in a way it is. My heart hurts from the strength of my response to his announcement, and the truth of what that means hits me.

I never want to say goodbye to Richard Hunter.

Chapter Twenty-Two

Richard

Maybe I've chosen the exact wrong moment to spring that announcement on Maddie. I do need to go home, but I don't want to leave her. Yes, I talked her into the idea of two weeks with no strings, and then we say goodbye. But the time I've spent with Maddie has been the happiest of my life, and I want it to go on forever, here on this enchanted island with this sweet, wonderful woman. It can't go on forever, though. I have responsibilities that I've ignored for too long.

I'd love to blame sex for distracting me, but until a few minutes ago, we hadn't shagged since that first night. The second I'd spoken the words, telling Maddie I need to leave, I'd experienced a strange discomfort, not quite a pain, not quite nausea.

Maddie sits up, strapping her arms around herself. "You're leaving? Just like that?"

"Not 'just like that.' I'd never planned to stay this long, but I extended my visit because of you." I sit up too and force myself to look into her eyes while I explain. "Now that I know Dexter wants to sign with my company, I don't need to be in the Caribbean anymore. I'll draft a contract from here, so I can have Dexter sign before I leave. But my company needs me. I've ignored work for too long, and I need to straighten things out back there."

"I get it." She whisks her hands up and down her arms, hugging herself tighter.

Maddie looks so…dejected. I want to hug her, but after what I've told her, I'm not sure she'll want me to do that. I'm feeling the way she looks, my shoulders caving in and an ice-cold lump forming in my gut.

"Where do you live?" I ask. "Can't believe I've never asked you that, but I just realized I haven't done. So where do you live, Maddie?"

"Nowhere." She hunches her shoulders. "I had an apartment in Chicago, but I was gone so much that I only went there maybe once a year. I gave up the lease so somebody else could have it. My job takes me all over the place, which means I haven't really had a home in years. My parents moved to Sweden several years ago, and my sister lives in England now. I'm a vagabond, I guess."

Her voice conveys a loneliness I hadn't noticed in her before. I suppose she's hidden it because we were virtual strangers when we met, and we've only just gotten better acquainted. I can't blame her for not sharing her deepest feelings with me. Maybe on some level, I sensed her loneliness, and that's why I've thought of her as a kindred spirit since the day we met. I've felt the way she looks right now. We've both let work take over our lives to the detriment of everything else.

Maddie's family lives closer to my home than to America, especially Rika. That realization prompts an idea, one I'm sure will be blown to bits once I voice it out loud. Maddie won't do it. How can she? We've known each other for less than two weeks.

She's gone quiet, her head down, her hands slack on her lap.

"If you need a place to stay," I begin, "I may have an option for you."

"You'll let me keep this suite for a while after you leave?"

"No." My mouth has suddenly gotten so dry that my tongue feels like a lump of wool. I glance at the palm trees, the sand, the surf, even my feet, before I order myself to stop acting like a coward and tell her what I want. I clear my throat. "Come home with me, Maddie. To England."

She jerks her head up, pinning her wide gaze on me. "What?"

"Come home with me. You said you have nowhere to go back to, and your sister lives not far from where I do, so…" I take her hands in mine. "Please come back to England with me. I can't say goodbye to you yet."

Though I'm not at all sure I can ever say goodbye to her, it's too soon to tell her that. Scaring her with a ridiculous, if heartfelt, declaration won't convince her to follow me home. I need her with me. Am I falling in love with her? I don't know for sure, but I wouldn't mind at all if I am.

I'm not stupid enough to blurt that out, though. Not yet. Wait until we're not ensconced in a tropical paradise where everything seems like heaven. Wait how long? Days? Weeks? I don't know how much longer I'll be able to hide my growing feelings for her. Not for weeks. Days might be a stretch too.

Maddie smiles in the sweetest way. "Yes, Richard, I would love to go home with you."

"Brilliant!" Do I shout that like a ruddy moron? Possibly. I'm too old to act like a lovestruck teenager, but I can't disguise how happy I am that she said yes. I drag her into my arms and kiss her. When I finally give up her lips, I say, "Let's skim through the rest of Dexter's books, then I'll draft a contract and call Ilsa. We may need to fly back to Dex's island, but I'm hoping I can take you home sometime tomorrow."

"I love that plan. Do I get to meet your family?"

"Why wouldn't you?"

"Don't know. You might feel weird about introducing me to your family since we met last week. This was supposed to be a vacation fling."

"But it's much more than that now." I pull her close again. "My parents will love you."

"My parents will love you too. Rika's already been telling them about you as part of her matchmaking scheme. She had Mom and Dad convinced you're my soul mate before we ever laid eyes on each other."

No one has ever made me feel as good as Maddie does. But soul mates? I don't know if I believe in that.

We go back to the resort to order dinner, then eat in our suite while skimming through Dexter's manuscripts. I'd known after reading one of his new books that I need to publish all of them. Even a quick browse of the others solidifies my commitment to this project. These eight novels are the best things he has ever written, and though they are a bit different from his previous books, I know the public will love the new novels. Each tells the story of one member of a large family. Every book can stand on its own, but the way they interweave makes the entire series so bloody good that I have trouble sticking to my plan to skim them so I can finish quickly.

At three o'clock in the morning, I finish the last page of the last book.

Maddie is lying beside me on the bed, asleep on her stomach.

She read one more book before she dozed off, and I read all the rest. My eyes are gritty and hot, but I don't care. I pull a Maddie trick, though for different reasons, and rifle through her purse to find a bottle of moisturizing eyedrops. I pour those into my eyes until I feel like I can look at a computer screen without going cross-eyed, then I draft a contract for Dexter. My company has a standard contract, so all I need to do is adjust some of the details to tailor it to this project. By the time I've emailed the contract to Ilsa, the sun is up.

I glance at the bedside clock. It's six a.m.

Maddie is still sleeping, her lips curled in the faintest smile.

She's so lovely. Just watching her sleep gives me a dull pain in my chest, but it feels good instead of unsettling.

A chime sounds, indicating one of us has a new text message.

It doesn't sound like my mobile, but I check it anyway. No, I don't have a text. So I grab Maddie's mobile and turn on the screen, intending only to glance at it to see if she has a text. She does, but it's displayed on the main screen. "Have you decided yet?" someone called Naveen asks. I glance at Maddie, at her sweet, sleeping face.

Another chime. Another text.

I fight the urge to read it, but I seem to have lost my mind in the past three seconds because I look at the screen again. This time Naveen says, "Miss you, babe." And then he includes a kissing-face emoji. This must be her former lover, the one she met in Somalia. But why is he kissing her via text message? She said they aren't together anymore.

Maddie rouses, sighing with contentment, and stretches her entire body. She yawns, opening her eyes. "Good morning. Sorry I fell asleep and left you to read all those books."

"Don't worry about that." I scratch my cheek, grimacing. "I, ah, sort of did a…bad thing."

She flips onto her back and laughs. "You being naughty? What a shocker."

I know she's obliquely referring to when we had sex last night, but I can't manage a smile. I keep grimacing. "I read your texts."

"You mean Dexter's books? Yeah, I know. I fell asleep and left you to do all the work."

"No, I don't mean that." I scrub my hands over my face and groan. "I heard a noise, like one of us had a text, but it wasn't my mobile. It was yours. And I inadvertently read those messages. Sorry."

"Messages? I have more than one text?" She sits up and checks her mobile. Her lips twist like she's trying not to smile, and she rotates her eyes to glance at me. "You read what Naveen said. That's the awful thing you did."

"Yes. I invaded your privacy."

She sets her mobile on the table, turns toward me, and… smiles. "You're adorable, Rick. I stole your wallet on the night we met so I could find out your name. You accidentally reading my texts is nothing."

"I might have accidentally read the first one, but I did it on purpose the second time."

"And I'm still not mad about that." She grasps my face and plants a firm but brief kiss on my mouth. "We're involved, right? I mean, you're taking me home with you, so we're not just two people having a fling anymore. That means you can check my phone if I get a call or a text and I'm…indisposed at the time." She bites her lip. "Was I snoring again?"

"No. You were a silent, delicate angel slumbering beside me."

"You are so full of shit."

"Maybe, but you are lovely when you're sleeping." I hesitate, not sure if it's my place to ask the next question, but she did say we're involved and I can answer her mobile whenever it's appropriate. So I go on and ask. "Is Naveen the man you were involved with?"

"Yeah, and he's also my coworker. Or he used to be." The second I open my mouth to speak again, she holds up a hand to stop me. "But no, I am not with him anymore, and I don't want to be.

Maybe he wants that, but I'm over it. That emoji is his problem, not mine."

"Good. I might've been slightly jealous when I saw that, but I'm not anymore."

My mobile rings. This time I'm sure it's mine because the screen tells me it's Ilsa calling.

"Good morning, Ilsa," I say when I pick up. "I assume you've seen the contract I sent."

"Sir Dexter and I have both reviewed it. He is ready to sign." When Ilsa is talking business, she always refers to her employer as Sir Dexter.

"He doesn't want to have his solicitor look it over first?" I ask.

"Sir Dexter does not believe in lawyers," she says. "He hates them even more than he hates agents and publishers, but he likes you and trusts you. We will arrive in twenty-five minutes to sign the contract."

"Dexter is coming here? To the resort?"

"That's correct. We will see you soon."

We say goodbye and end the call.

I face Maddie. "Dexter is coming to see us. We have twenty-five minutes to get ready."

"Twenty-five minutes?" Maddie almost shrieks. She flies off the bed, scrambling to find and open her suitcase. While she frantically searches inside it for the right clothes, she starts babbling. "I need a shower, but is there enough time? I haven't eaten breakfast yet either. Oh God, what if I have dark circles under my eyes? Where's my makeup bag?"

"I need a shower too. Let's save time by doing that together."

"Oh great. Like I'll get clean if we shower together."

"You have my solemn word that I will not shag you."

She's clutching a pile of clothes to her chest, but when she looks at me, she isn't as manic as she was a minute ago. "Okay, fine. We'll take a shower together." She manages to wag a finger at me while still clutching her clothes in both arms. "No sex, Rick. None whatsoever."

"I promise."

And I fulfill that vow. The shower is so large that we could stand five feet apart and still have room left. We don't stand that far apart, but I do keep my hands off her. While she blow-dries her hair and does whatever else women do to prepare for the day, I get dressed and print out the contract. I also arrange for a flight home for me and Maddie. We'll fly to the UK later today.

I order breakfast too, making sure to order enough that Ilsa and Dexter can have some, in case they haven't eaten yet.

Maddie emerges from the bathroom just as someone knocks on the door.

The second I open the door, Dexter throws his arms around me. He thumps both hands on my back repeatedly. "Wonderful news, Rick, wonderful news."

"What is?"

He releases me but keeps his hands on my shoulders. "The contract, of course. What else? You're the perfect man to publish my books." He tips his head in Maddie's direction. "I knew your excellent taste in women meant you have excellent taste overall."

Dexter hugs Maddie too, and Ilsa kisses my cheek. She hugs Maddie, but not as boisterously as Dex had done.

He signs the contract before we eat, then we all enjoy a meal together while we exchange jokes and talk about Dexter's new books. Once the food is gone, Maddie and I tell him how much we love the stories, and I comment on the differences between these books and his old ones, particularly the family element.

Dexter slips an arm around Ilsa's shoulders, giving her a gentle squeeze. His expression becomes softer, full of genuine affection. "Family means even more to me today than it did in the old days. I had a son with my second wife, but we've grown apart. We still talk, but we're not especially close. When Ilsa came into my life, everything changed."

Ilsa gazes at him with a tender smile curving her lips.

He kisses her forehead. "Ilsa is my daughter. I never knew about her until five years ago when she sought me out. I'd had a fling with her mother, after my first wife divorced me but before I married my second wife. I never saw Greta again after our one night together, and she never let me know I have a child." He kisses Ilsa's cheek. "My daughter is the light of my life, and the inspiration for the family saga I've written."

"You wrote all these books since you met Ilsa?" I ask.

"That's right. I was inspired." He stands up, and so does Ilsa. "Time for us to go home. Thank you, Richard, for agreeing to publish these books. I wish everyone could experience the kind of joy Ilsa has brought me, and I hope these books will accomplish that in some small way."

"You should come to the UK sometime. For a visit, not publicity."

"What a smashing idea. Ilsa and I would love that."

Ilsa lays a hand on her chest, feigning a shocked expression. "Richard, you've performed a miracle. You have cured my father of his misanthropic ways."

"Don't exaggerate, love," Dexter tells her. "I don't hate all people. Only publishers and literary agents." He slaps my arm. "Present company excluded."

We all say goodbye—and it's time for me and Maddie to go home. Will she want to stay for long? I have no idea, but I plan to do whatever I can to convince her to stay forever.

On the long journey back to the UK, we talk about everything except our feelings for each other. The need to tell her how much she means to me grows inside me, the pressure urging me to confess. But there's a certain someone she's going to meet tomorrow, and I haven't told her about him yet, so I'll hold off on confessing my feelings until I see how she reacts to Nick. I should warn her about my brother, but I'm too busy enjoying these last hours of solitude with Maddie. Though it will be early evening when we arrive in the UK, we both need to sleep before I introduce her to everyone. We'll drive to my home in Colchester to rest up, then tomorrow, the throng will descend—my family, her sister, the Dixons, and whoever else they invite.

Can I handle it if Maddie takes one look at my brother and decides he's more exciting than I am? I can't believe she will, but my brother knows how to charm women, and they always love his career choice.

Tomorrow, I'll find out if she wants only my face and my voice, or if what she feels for me is really about me.

Chapter Twenty-Three

Maddie

I don't feel jet-lagged this morning, but then, sleeping with Richard Hunter always makes me feel relaxed and refreshed. After our whirlwind romance and our whirlwind trip to the UK, plus our whirlwind drive from London to Colchester, I'd needed lots of rest. Most people sleep on the plane, but we talked instead. So yeah, I conked out the second my head hit the pillow. I slept for twelve hours.

This morning, I'm lying in Rick's bed while he snores this time. He looks so adorable spread out on his tummy, with his head turned to the side, his mouth open, and his hair a mess. He's naked too. So am I. We didn't have sex last night, though. We undressed and collapsed onto the bed, too exhausted to bother digging through our bags to find our sleeping clothes.

The sheet has slipped off Rick's ass.

Naturally, I ogle him. He has a great ass, and I have no willpower or desire to keep myself from admiring that part of him at length. He shouldn't sleep on his tummy if he doesn't want me to drool over his tight bottom.

After a while, I get tired of waiting for him to wake up. So I crawl half on top of him and kiss my way up his backside, starting with those fine glutes and following a trail up to his cheek. The other kind of cheek, the one on his face. When I place a firm kiss on his lips, his lids flutter open.

He blinks rapidly, scrunching up his face. "Maddie?"

"Uh-huh. Who else did you think would be crawling up your naked body?" I nibble on his chin. "Good morning, Rick."

Yawning, he tries to roll over but realizes he can't move because I'm on top of him. His lips curve into a sleepy, but still damn sexy, smile. "Good morning, Maddie."

I lay an open-mouth kiss on his shoulder. "You better have food around here because I'm starved. I might eat you if I don't get some actual food soon. Well, I'll probably devour you anyway."

"And I'd love for you to do that." He wriggles until I slide off him, then he turns onto his side. "Are you ready to meet my family today? The Dixons will be here too. My parents are good friends with their parents, and when I told Mum I was coming home—with my new girlfriend—she announced we need to have a big do. I normally don't like parties, but since I met you, I want all sorts of things I never wanted before."

"And a party is one of those things."

"We need to celebrate our relationship and the good news for my company."

"Absolutely." I sit up, stretching. "But first, we need breakfast."

We get dressed, then Rick makes me a delicious breakfast. After that, we have sex. Big surprise, right? We can't keep our hands off each other, but we also love cuddling and talking while we cuddle. Eventually, we have to get up and get dressed, again, so we can head over to the big house where the parents of the Dixon brothers live. Rick has a beautiful house, but it's not large, and he doesn't have the outdoor furniture to accommodate his friends and relatives. He can afford to buy a mansion, like one of those historic ones with five floors and umpteen rooms. But he told me he doesn't like huge houses.

I don't think I'd like living in a mansion either.

We arrive before everyone else—except, of course, the Dixons' parents since we're going to their house—but Richard's parents show up not long after us. They both hug me and say how happy they are that their son finally found the right woman. Rick points out we met two weeks ago, but they don't care.

"You haven't been serious about a girl in ages," Rick's father, Edward, says. "It's about time you settled down. We need grandchildren."

Children? Sheesh, we only admitted yesterday that we want more than a fling with each other.

But Edward is smiling, and his eyes are twinkling, so I figure he's not seriously expecting us to have a baby next week.

His wife, Pippa, clasps her hands under her chin, smiling too. "Oh Rick, I thought you'd never get married."

Married? Well, at least she didn't jump straight to grandkids. Mrs. Hunter will probably ally with my sister to start planning the wedding this afternoon.

Richard's parents are such nice people, though, that I can't be offended by anything they say. They're thrilled their son has a girlfriend, and I'm too happy to let anything unsettle me.

Do I love him? Too soon to tell. At least I now have a place to stay, but I still don't know what I'm going to do with my life. I want to be with Rick, but that's all I can say for sure. My vagabond lifestyle is all I've known for years, and it's hard to break a habit. I don't want to go anywhere, though, not without Richard Hunter.

His brother still hasn't arrived. Richard hasn't told me much at all about Nick, which only awakens the insatiable curiosity of Dr. Solberg.

I'm relaxing on a lawn chair, the kind that lets me stretch my legs out, and admiring the gorgeous, flowering bushes when the rest of the guests arrive. I hear them inside the house laughing. Richard went in there a few minutes ago to wait for his friends and his brother to show up, but he encouraged me to stay out here and "enjoy the quiet while it lasts."

Having met the Dixons, I know this will be one raucous party, especially with Reese Dixon on the premises. He's tons of fun. Rick is tons of fun too but in a different way. He's not as boisterous as Reese, and he's much less likely to make a raunchy joke.

Like I said, I'm sitting here gazing at the flowers, not paying attention to anything else.

A shadow falls over me, and I glance at the man standing beside my chair.

"Not going to ogle me from the front again?" I ask. "You're trying the sneaky side attack this time."

Though he's wearing slacks and a long-sleeve dress shirt, he sits down on the concrete patio beside me, much the way he'd sat next to my beach chair on the day we met. His shiny shoes and his clothes look nothing like what he wore back then. I'm still half-convinced he sprayed those swim briefs onto his body.

"I've been talking to your sister," he says.

"Let me guess. She's telling everyone I'm a combination of Marie Curie and Wonder Woman."

"No, but I was less interested in what she said than the way she said it."

I twist sideways in my chair to aim a sarcastically offended look at him. "Are you trying to make time with my baby sister?"

"Rika is lovely, but no." He smiles, and it's a mixture of sarcasm and smugness. "She sounds an awful lot like you. That's what I meant."

"Oh, I get it. This is your revenge for what I said about how your voice sounds a lot like Alex, the Dixons, and Dexter."

"I believe you said all Brits have the same smooth voices, and you suggested I have some bloke in my head telling me what to say."

"No, you suggested all you Brits' voices are narrated by one man. I mentioned that movie about a guy who hears a writer's words in his head."

"Hmm." He bends one knee to rest his arm on it, regarding me with a devious glint in his eyes. "Not only do you sound very much like Rika, but you both have voices quite like Elena's and Arden's. Maybe you lot have one woman narrating for you."

"Don't be ridiculous. I sound nothing like Elena or Arden."

"I see. There's a double standard, eh? I'm shocked at your lack of scientific rigor in this matter."

He's smirking now, and I'm such a sucker for this guy that I love his sarcastic smile and his silly attempt to convince me that I sound like Elena and Arden, the wives of Chance and Reese Dixon. I'm right about his voice, but he is absolutely wrong about mine. Am I applying a double standard here? No, never, not me. Okay, *maybe* I am.

Rick rubs his chin like he's giving his idea serious thought. "Maybe I should run a two-arm parallel assignment to prove my point."

"Do you even remember what that means?"

His mouth slides into a sexy grin. "Not a fucking clue."

I roll my eyes to emphasize the sarcasm in my tone. "Oh, now that's *very* scientific."

Rick watches me for a moment without speaking, and all the humor vacates his expression.

"Are you okay?" I ask. "I was just teasing you."

"I'm not offended." He bows his head. "I want to tell you something, but I'm afraid it might sound insane."

"You can tell me anything."

He swallows hard enough that I can see his Adam's apple jumping. Then he licks his lips but in a nervous way instead of a sexy one. Finally, he shoves a hand into his hair and clears his throat, his gaze aimed straight into mine. "I love you, Maddie."

"I love you too." The words pour out of me before I realize what I'm about to say. Once I've spoken those four syllables, I can't believe I've said them. But I'm not embarrassed or freaked out by it. I meant those words. I love Richard Hunter.

"You do?" he asks, sounding baffled. "We've known each other for not quite two weeks. I assumed you'd think I'm barmy if I told you how I feel."

"I don't think that. And I didn't fully understand how I feel until you said that, then I couldn't stop myself from saying it back. I know this thing between us happened fast, but I also know it's real. I love you, Rick."

He rises to his knees and leans in to kiss me.

By the time he's done doing that, I feel warm and soft and blissfully satisfied.

"Have you decided about that job in Atlanta?" he asks.

"Oh yeah. Sorry, I forgot to tell you. I texted Naveen yesterday morning while you were still asleep and told him I appreciate the offer but it's not right for me."

"What did he say?"

"That he understands, and he wishes me well."

"So, what will you do now?"

"Don't know. I'll figure that out later." I lay a hand on his cheek. "Today, I just want to have fun with you and your friends and your family. Speaking of family, when do I get to meet the mysterious Nick?"

One corner of his mouth slants upward. "Soon, I promise. But first, I need to go inside and check on something."

"I'll come with you."
"No. This is a…private matter. You'll understand in a little while."
He stands, kisses my forehead, and walks away.
What is that sneaky, sexy man up to?

Chapter Twenty-Four

Richard

I hover at the edge of the patio, a few meters behind Maddie's chair, not speaking to make sure she doesn't know I'm here. I've orchestrated a surprise for her, one I think she'll appreciate. She loves to tease me, so I'm going to tease her. Or rather, get my mate to tease her on my behalf.

Alex Thorne stands beside me, his gaze shifting back and forth between me and Maddie. He keeps his voice soft enough that she won't hear. "Are you sure about this? You know I'm game for anything, but you don't strike me as the practical-joke sort."

"Maybe I haven't been until now, until I met Maddie."

"The right woman can completely alter your perspective. Though I have to wonder about Maddie's mental state in light of her potty theory about us."

"She was joking. I think."

"Let's hope so." He claps a hand on my shoulder. "Shall we do this?"

"Yes, go on. You're up first."

Alex nods, then he approaches Maddie's chair, halting just behind it.

She's engrossed in studying the bushes or something, so she doesn't notice.

I move closer, though not too close or she might spot me.

Alex leans in to cover her eyes with his hands. "Hungry for a kiss, Luscious?"

She contorts her mouth into an expression I've come to know as Maddie thinking. I can't see her eyes, but I'm sure she's squinting them. Her brows have lowered too. Gradually, her lips curve into a sexily teasing smile. "Oh yes, I'd love to make out with you, Alex. I'm sure Rick won't mind at all."

Alex removes his hands from her eyes and glances at me, shrugging.

Maddie tips her head back to peer up at him.

"Clever girl," Alex says. "Rick was sure you wouldn't be fooled, but I hoped calling you Luscious might confuse you a little."

"Nice try, but I spent a week with the Dixons before they shipped me off to the Caribbean for a matchmaking vacation. I know Reese calls his wife Luscious. Besides, I might think you Brits all have similarly smooth voices, but I know who's who when I hear you guys talking."

"Now I understand why Rick fell under your spell. You're even cleverer than I expected, Dr. Solberg."

She cranes her neck around to see me. "Richard Hunter, you naughty man, playing a trick like that. You're testing me, aren't you?"

I amble over to her chair and kneel beside it, giving her a quick kiss. "It wasn't a test. It was payback for your claim that I sound like the Dixons, Alex Thorne, and Dexter Armstrong-Hill."

Alex is still standing behind her chair smirking.

"You can bugger off now," I tell him. "Your services are no longer needed."

"If you need help with Maddie again, I'm always available. In whatever capacity you need me to fulfill."

"No thank you, Alex. I fulfill every capacity that Madeleine requires."

The cheeky arse walks away.

I take hold of Maddie's hands and help her get up. "Lunch is almost ready."

"Great. I'm famished."

"But I have another surprise for you first. To complete my two-arm parallel assignment."

"You really shouldn't use that term since you have no clue what it means." She pats my cheek. "But it's adorable that you're trying to use my scientific terms."

I step away from her, creating a gap of several feet between us. "Close your eyes, Maddie. I have one more test for you, and it was my brother's idea."

"He's finally here? I've been waiting to meet him."

"Now you can. But close your eyes first."

She does what I asked.

I wave at the person who waits just outside the door to the house. My brother strides over to us, flashes me a snarky smile, then leans in close to Maddie. He blows a breath over her lips.

That was not part of the plan. I want to tell him to bugger off, except that would ruin our little test.

But I do scowl at him.

Nick grins and winks, enjoying this game a bit too much for my taste. His mouth is far too close to Maddie's when he speaks. "Do you still think all British men sound the same? Maybe I should kiss you to make sure this test is thorough."

Did his lips brush against hers? I think they did. The sod seems to be trying it on with my girlfriend. And why has he made his voice lower and huskier like he really is trying it on with Maddie?

No, he's not doing that. I'm an arsehole for thinking it. Nick might be more like Reese Dixon than like me, but he's not a girlfriend thief. This is the first time I've introduced Maddie to my brother or any of my family, so of course, I'm a tiny bit anxious about having her meet Nick. For our entire relationship until today, we'd been sequestered on a Caribbean island. Coming home feels good, but also strange. And I have no idea how she'll react to my brother.

"Well, Maddie?" Nick asks with his mouth still much closer to hers than necessary. "Should I give you a big, hot, wet kiss?"

"Nice try, but I know you're Nick."

"You know?" He backs away from her, shaking his head. "I suppose my impersonation of Rick wasn't very convincing. It's hard to talk like a businessman who has a stick permanently shoved up his arse."

"Can I open my eyes now?"

I open my mouth to say yes.

But my brother intervenes. "Not yet. One more small test. One of us is going to kiss you."

"Like hell you're kissing Maddie," I say, grabbing Nick's arm to drag him farther away from her. "She's my girlfriend. Get your own."

"How did you find your soul mate before I found mine? I'm much more entertaining than you."

"Yes, you and Reese love to harass me and the other mature men in the room." When Nick tries to move closer to Maddie, I slap a hand on his chest to stop him. "The test is over. Open your eyes, Maddie."

She does that, and her jaw drops. "But you—your faces—holy shit." She smacks my arm, much harder than I'd slapped Nick's chest. "You rat. Why didn't you tell me you have a twin brother?"

Nick slaps a hand on my shoulder. "He's embarrassed because I'm the one the ladies love. Rick has always had his nose in a book while I was chasing skirts."

Maddie glances at me. "Rick does just fine with the ladies."

"I'm a massage therapist," my brother announces. "That means I know all the best ways to touch a woman."

"Piss off, Nick," I say, elbowing him out of the way.

He raises his hands, palms out. "All right, Rick, settle down. Naturally, you're sensitive about blokes talking to your girl. She's the first one you've ever brought home to meet Mum and Dad."

Maddie blinks at me. "Is that true?"

"Yes, it is."

"Don't be embarrassed. I'm honored to be the first."

She's smiling at me sweetly, and I know she means that.

The three of us go inside the house for lunch. Luckily, the Dixon elders have a large dining room with a long table that fits all of us. Nick wants to sit beside Maddie, and I consider saying no, but then I realize I'm being a ruddy arse again. Besides, I want Maddie to get to know my brother. Despite his sometimes-annoying behavior, I love Nick. We are twins, after all, so he's a part of my life no matter where I go.

Nick and I sit on either side of Maddie.

Reese Dixon and Alex Thorne wind up seated directly across the table from us, so Maddie is treated to plenty of naughty jokes and innuendo. Maddie can dish it out as well as they can, and she seems to love the banter. Since she keeps massaging my thigh under the table, I know she's not at all interested in those other blokes.

After lunch, we excuse ourselves, saying we need to go back to my house and rest. It's jet lag, you know.

We don't sleep, though. We shag. Repeatedly.

For the next two weeks, Maddie spends a lot of time with my parents and Nick while I manage my company from the comfort of home so I can be with my family and Maddie too. I've delegated the task of preparing Dexter's manuscripts for release to my editor-in-chief, a man I trust implicitly. He's been with the company since before I took over for my father. We settle the lawsuit Miriam Watkins filed against our company, and I inject my own money into the deal to sweeten the settlement.

At least it's over now.

Things aren't as bad for my company as I'd feared they would be in the aftermath of the lawsuit. I've signed a new author who I know will never commit copyright infringement. Alex Thorne has written a terrific book about sexual practices throughout ancient history, and I have a feeling *Dirty-Sexy Archaeology* will be a winner. An honest winner. No cheating necessary. With Alex and Dexter signed with Hunter Publishing, the future looks bright indeed.

I take Maddie to London with me for the press conference where I'll make the big announcement about Dexter's books. No one is talking about that silly reality star or her lawsuit. They're applauding the biggest publishing deal in decades and buzzing about what Dexter's new novels will be like. Maddie suggests I should put at least one of Dexter's books up for preorder right now, at least in ebook format, so everyone can order while the buzz is still hot. I doubt any traditional publisher has ever slapped a book up for preorder faster than my team does when I give the order.

And the sales flood in. It's already turning into the biggest success my company has ever seen.

Maddie and I stay in London for a few days, taking a mini holiday to celebrate…everything. When we return to Colchester, I decide I've waited long enough to ask the question I now realize I've wanted to ask for as long as I've known Maddie. I delayed only because it felt insane to move this fast, but I don't care any-more. No more overthinking. I'm going to do what feels right—and for the first time in my life, I know what that is.

I take Maddie out into the garden at my home, where blooms of all colors surround us, though their beauty can't compare to Mad-die's. When I drop to one knee, she smiles—and I know she knows what I'm about to do.

"Madeleine, I love you," I tell her as I hold both her hands. "I don't care that we've only known each other for a few weeks—"

"Four weeks and two days."

"Precision isn't critical here." I gaze up into her blue eyes. "Will you marry me, Maddie?"

"Yes, of course I will."

That's all I need to hear. I pull her into my arms and kiss her.

I thought I didn't have time for a relationship, but Maddie Sol-berg proved me wrong.

My fiancée receives good news of her own later in the day. She's been offered a part-time teaching position at a university in Lon-don, which leaves her with plenty of time to keep up her disease-detective work too, on a freelance basis from the comfort of our home in Colchester.

When we have our engagement party a few days later, Maddie's sister and her husband spend more time with us than even my par-ents and brother do. Rika is very happy—thrilled might be a better word for it—that Maddie is getting married. Rika keeps glancing at my brother so frequently that I finally have to ask her.

"Why are you staring at Nick?"

Rika swerves her attention to me, fluttering her lashes like she's confused or has something in her eyes, then she smiles and laughs. "Maddie and I have been talking about your brother."

"Why? If you want a free massage, I'm sure Nick would love to give you one."

"Like hell he will," Dane Dixon declares. "I'm the only one who gives my wife a massage."

Rika snuggles up to her husband. "Relax, baby, that's not what Maddie and I were discussing."

"Then what were you talking about?" I ask.

"What to do about Nick."

I'm not sure what she means, but I have a sneaking suspicion. "What exactly do you think needs to be done for him?"

Rika curls her lips into a knowing smile. "He's single, so we're going to find him a girlfriend."

Won't Nick love that? I think these women need a hobby—other than matchmaking.

Later, when Maddie and I are crawling under the covers together, she reintroduces the topic.

"Nick needs to settle down, don't you think? He's so cute and nice."

"Don't try to rope me into the matchmaking scheme you and your sister dreamed up."

"I won't. But you have to admit, Rika's meddling worked for us."

"And I'm grateful for that, but please stay out of my brother's love life."

Maddie slips her arm and her leg over my body, her head nestled against my neck. "I will. But there's no stopping Rika now. She's on a mission, and Arden and Elena have signed on to her plan."

Since I'm quite sure I don't want to know their plan, I roll us both over so I'm on top of Maddie, then I make love to her.

As for Nick...Well, he's about to find out what lengths these determined American women will go to in the name of love.

Did you wonder what the deal is with Maddie insisting Richard sounds a lot like his British pals? It's a little inside joke for fans of my audiobooks. Narrator Shane East has taken on the role of the hero in each Hot Brits book as well as playing the British hero in *Irresistible in a Kilt* (part of the Hot Scots series). Vanessa Edwin has performed the heroines' roles in the Hot Brits series, so that's why Richard gets his revenge by suggesting Maddie sounds like those other American ladies.

I hope you enjoyed these humorous moments in *One Hot Escape*, and if you haven't listened to the audio versions of these stories, maybe you'll want to now. Shane and Vanessa are amazing!

Thank you for reading *One Hot Escape*!

Anna Durand is a bestselling, multi-award-winning author of contemporary and paranormal romance. Her books have earned bestseller status on every major retailer and wonderful reviews from readers around the world. But that's the boring spiel. Here are the really cool things you want to know about Anna!

Born on Lachland Air Force Base in Texas, Anna grew up moving here, there, and everywhere thanks to her dad's job as an instructor pilot. She's lived in Texas (twice), Mississippi, California (twice), Michigan (twice), and Alaska—and now Ohio.

As for her writing, Anna has always made up stories in her head, but she didn't write them down until her teen years. Those first awful books went into the trash can a few years later, though she learned a lot from those stories. Eventually, she would pen her first romance novel, the paranormal romance *Willpower*, and she's never looked back since.

Want even more details about Anna? Get access to her extended bio when you subscribe to her newsletter and download the free bonus ebook, *Hot Scots Confidential*. You'll also get hot deleted scenes, character interviews, fun facts, and more! Plus you'll receive the short story *Tempted by a Kiss*, two bonus chapters for *One Hot Chance*, and a bonus audiobook chapter narrated for you by Shane East.

Visit AnnaDurand.com to sign up.